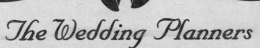

The Wedding Planners

Planning perfect weddings...
finding happy endings!

It's the biggest and most important day of a
woman's life—and it has to be perfect.

At least that's what the Wedding Belles believe, and
that's why they're Boston's top wedding-planner
agency. But amidst the beautiful bouquets, divine
dresses and rose-petal confetti, these six wedding
planners long to be planning their own big day!

But first they have to find Mr. Right....

This month:
SOS Marry Me!
by Melissa McClone

Designer: Serena's already made her dress,
but a rebel has won her heart....

And don't miss the exciting
wedding-planner tips and author
reminiscences that accompany each book!

Melissa spills the beans about her own wedding dress:

"I was a practical bride on a budget—a mechanical engineer who couldn't conceive of spending tons of money on a dress I would wear only once. But there was a secret romantic in me, a woman who wrote romance novels on her lunch hour and dreamed of feeling, for one special day, like Grace Kelly or Princess Diana or Cinderella.

Never mind, I told myself firmly as I went shopping. It's only one day. It's only one dress.

I visited store after store. I found practical gowns. Budget-priced gowns. I tried on dress after dress. And staring in the mirror, I never saw the bride of my romantic longings smiling back at me.

Nearing desperation, I went to a bridal boutique a coworker had recommended. The gowns I tried on were far from practical, and not one was on sale. But finally, as I was zipped and hooked and buttoned into what must have been my hundredth dress, I turned to the mirror and saw…a bride. Me. The girl of my romantic dreams. The woman who was ready to pledge her life to one special man.

Only one day. Only one dress.

I bought it.

As I wrote *SOS Marry Me!*, I thought about the friend who helped me find my gown and the woman who designed it. She knew what was important to brides. And so does my wedding-dress-designer heroine, Serena James.

Hear all about Melissa's latest news at www.melissamcclone.com And for more wedding fun check out www.harlequin-theweddingplanners.blogspot.com.

MELISSA MCCLONE

SOS Marry Me!

The
Wedding
Planners

HARLEQUIN®

TORONTO • NEW YORK • LONDON
AMSTERDAM • PARIS • SYDNEY • HAMBURG
STOCKHOLM • ATHENS • TOKYO • MILAN • MADRID
PRAGUE • WARSAW • BUDAPEST • AUCKLAND

For my own Belles: Shirley Jump, Myrna Mackenzie, Linda Goodnight, Susan Meier and Melissa James. Talented Harlequin authors and amazing friends!

Special thanks to: Missoula County Detective David Brenner, Idaho County Sheriff Larry Dasenbrock, Virendra Gauthier, John Frieh, Virginia Kantra, Michael Leming, Dru Ann Love, Mike Mooney, Anne Ryan, Tiffany Talbott and last, but not least, Carol Hennessey, Jen Hensiek and Le Ann Martin with the Clearwater National Forest.
I take full responsibility for any mistakes and/or discrepancies!

ISBN-13: 978-0-373-17519-2
ISBN-10:   0-373-17519-1

SOS MARRY ME!

First North American Publication 2008.

www.eHarlequin.com

Printed in U.S.A.

Planning perfect weddings...finding happy endings!

In April: *Sweetheart Lost and Found*
by Shirley Jump
*Florist: Will Callie catch a bouquet
and reunite with her childhood sweetheart?*

In May: *The Heir's Convenient Wife*
by Myrna Mackenzie
*Photographer: Regina's wedding album is perfect.
Now she needs her husband to say I love you!*

In June: *SOS Marry Me!*
by Melissa McClone
*Designer: Serena's already made her dress,
but a rebel has won her heart.*

In July: *Winning the Single Mom's Heart*
by Linda Goodnight
Chef: Who will Natalie cut her own wedding cake with?

In August: *Millionaire Dad, Nanny Needed!*
by Susan Meier
*Accountant: Will Audra's budget for the big day
include a millionaire groom?*

In September: *The Bridegroom's Secret*
by Melissa James
*Planner: Julie's always been the wedding planner—
will she ever be the bride?*

Serena is a top wedding-dress designer for the Wedding Belles. Here are her tips on how to pick the right dress for your big day:

❦ Don't visit too many bridal boutiques on the same day. Trying on wedding gowns should be a fun experience, not a chore! Do invite a trusted friend or your mother to go with you to offer opinions and support. But try to discourage the entire bridal party from trooping along. Too many opinions may only confuse you. Ultimately, it's your day, your dress and your decision.

❦ Stark white, diamond white, ivory and champagne are a few of the "whites" used for wedding-dress fabrics. Try on different shades of white to determine which one flatters your skin tone and hair color best.

❦ Discuss the type of wedding you are having and your dress budget with the sales consultant before she brings you dresses to try on. If money is an issue, ask about bridesmaid dresses that can be worn as wedding gowns. They can be quite lovely, but less expensive.

❦ Try on all the gowns the sales consultant suggests. Dresses look very different on the hanger than on a bride. Don't forget that your dream gown might not fit your body type, so it's a good idea to try on a variety of styles to see how they look on you.

❦ Take at least two pairs of comfortable shoes with different heel heights to the final dress fitting. If the hem isn't exactly right, you won't freak out and you'll be good to go for your wedding day.

CHAPTER ONE

"I'LL go to the bridal show," Serena James announced. "I've always wanted to visit Seattle."

Not that she cared where she went as long as she could get out of town.

Four of her coworkers at The Wedding Belles, a Boston-based full-service wedding planning company, turned surprised looks in her direction. Oops. Serena tried not to grimace. Had she sounded too enthusiastic for a woman with a devoted boyfriend?

"That is, if no one else wants to go," she added with a forced smile.

"Well, darlin'," Belle Mackenzie, owner of The Wedding Belles, purred in her distinct Southern drawl. A beautiful woman with coiffed silver hair and a generous glossed smile, she gave the best hugs this side of the Mason-Dixon line. "That's sweet of you to offer. We do need a little positive publicity after the Vandiver wedding cancellation fiasco, and the show's sponsors would be delighted to have one of the country's up-and-coming wedding dress designers fill in at the last moment."

This was going to work. Satisfaction filled Serena.

"But you usually avoid bridal shows," Belle continued. "Are you sure about this with all you have going on?"

"I'm sure," Serena answered, hoping to sound willing but not desperate. "Besides, there really isn't anyone else."

Belle drummed her French-manicured nails on the mahogany table. "That's true. We all seem to have an extra serving or two on our plates."

"Well, whoever goes to Seattle—" Callie Underwood, florist extraordinaire, brushed a lock of dark blond hair off her face "—I want them to take my wedding gown to the show."

The other women gasped.

"You're getting married in just a few weeks," Belle said.

"November 22 to be exact, as Jared keeps reminding me, but we need to show brides that The Wedding Belles is still one of the premier wedding planning companies in the country, if not the world," Callie explained. "That means showing off what we do best, everything from Natalie's delicious cakes to Serena's stunning designs. Serena's entire spring line is beautiful, but my custom gown is her latest and most exquisite creation."

"But it's your wedding dress," Serena said. "I made it to fit you, not some size zero model. Anyway, I wouldn't want to risk getting makeup or runway stains on the silk."

"That doesn't mean you couldn't display the gown on a mannequin in the booth."

"What if something happens to the dress?" Regina O'Ryan, a gifted photographer, asked.

"Nothing will happen to it." Callie winked across the table. "Isn't that right, Serena?"

"Not if I'm the one who goes to Seattle." Serena appreciated her friend's vote of confidence. She wouldn't let Callie down. "I'll make sure the dress comes back."

"Seattle is on the other side of the country." Regina, her

brown eyes as bright as the flash on her ever-present camera, leaned toward her. "Did you and Rupert have plans for that weekend?"

Serena gritted her teeth at the mention of her boyfriend's—make that ex-boyfriend's—name, but her smile remained steadfast. "He's been traveling a lot himself. He won't mind."

At all.

She hadn't spoken to him in months. Not since he'd dumped her in April after The Wedding Belles' assistant, Julie Montgomery, had announced her engagement to Matt McLachlan. Serena still hadn't figured out how to tell people.

Things like this didn't happen to her. Serena lived a charmed life. She was used to getting what she wanted. She'd wanted to get married and start a family. She'd thought she'd found the right guy except that she'd been too focused on the end result to realize he hadn't been so right after all.

"We don't have any plans," she added.

"You got the last good man, Serena," Natalie Thompson, a young widow with mischievous eight-year-old twin girls, said. The petite blonde sighed. "After Julie, Callie and Regina. Pretty soon, we'll have another Belle's wedding to plan. I can already guess the cake you'll want. Chocolate with orange-flavored fudge filling."

The baker, who called herself a cake fairy, brought in slices for the Belles to try every time she made samples for brides to taste. That Natalie remembered her favorite flavor touched Serena.

"And I know the flowers." Callie's green eyes twinkled like the white mini decorator lights she used with yards of tulle and garlands of blossoms. "White dendrobium orchids, green roses, green cymbidium orchids and white and green parrot tulips."

White and green. One of Serena's favorite color combinations. She shouldn't be surprised. Callie knew her tastes so well.

A cake. Flowers. Serena's friends had her perfect wedding figured out. The only thing missing was…the groom.

A weight pressed down on the center of her chest. She thought of the nearly completed wedding dress hanging in her hall closet. Okay, she had been foolish, tempting fate by starting on the gown before she had a ring. But who could blame her?

Her relationship with Rupert Collier had proceeded right on schedule. They'd dated a year, met and liked each other's families and talked about the future, about creating a family together, which was what Serena wanted most of all. Becoming engaged had been the next obvious step. She'd started work on her wedding dress because she'd wanted time to get every stitch and every detail exactly right. She'd chosen the fabrics and design with the same care with which she'd chosen Rupert Collier. Not only smart, gorgeous and rich, but also ideal husband and father material. Everything she'd been looking for in a man, everything her friends expected her boyfriend to be, everything her parents wanted her to marry.

Until, impatient for a ring after dating exclusively for so long, she'd brought up the *M*-word. *Marriage*. And suddenly her perfect boyfriend wasn't ready for a serious relationship. He'd accused her of being too selfish and too self-reliant to make a permanent commitment. Oh he'd wanted to keep seeing her, she remembered bitterly. They looked good together and his boss liked her. But he'd wanted to take a serious step backward in the commitment department. Maybe, he'd suggested, they should start dating other people, too. Serena had said no, thinking he only needed a push to get their relationship back on track. Rupert had said goodbye. Proving once again that if she didn't do what others wanted, she wouldn't get what she wanted.

His parting words had stung.

You don't need me, Serena. You don't need anyone.

In the months since, she'd come to realize he was right. They were better off without each other. She didn't need him. She hadn't loved him the way a woman should love the man she wanted to marry. She hadn't wanted him as much as she liked how he'd fit into her plans. So much for her perfect dress. Her perfect groom. Her perfect life.

She forced herself to breathe. A setback, yes. A total failure, no. Serena James didn't fail.

Regina grinned, as if she'd found the perfect Kodak moment to capture with her camera. "Rupert will have to adjust his travel schedule once you get married."

Serena's stomach roiled. Her temples throbbed. She hated keeping secrets from the women she cared most about in the world, women who were more like family than coworkers, but what else was she supposed to do?

Julie had been thrilled about getting engaged. The other Belles were excited to be giving her a dream wedding. Serena couldn't let her bad news affect everyone else's joy. When Callie had fallen in love with Jared, Serena hadn't wanted her breakup to take anything away from the couple's happiness. And after Regina and Dell's marriage had become a love match, Serena couldn't find the right time to tell everyone she'd been dumped.

Now wasn't the right time, either.

Natalie and Audra Green, the company's accountant,

were down on men. Telling them the truth about what had happened would only reaffirm their belief that Mr. Right didn't exist. Serena wouldn't do that to her friends. They'd already faced too much disappointment and heartache.

Besides, her friends expected more from her. Everyone did. Serena worked hard on her polished image, kept a positive attitude and was always there in a pinch. People counted on her. They expected her to find Mr. Right.

That was exactly what she intended to do—find someone to give her the perfect love, family and life she dreamed about. Just because she'd been wrong about one man didn't mean her one true love wasn't out there somewhere. Maybe even in Seattle.

"So about the bridal show—" Serena leaned back in her chair "—what else do I need to bring with me in addition to the wedding dresses?"

Kane Wiley ducked around the business jet's engine to place his bags in the plane's exterior storage compartment. His breath steamed in the November air.

"Is that all you've got?" his father, Charlie, asked.

"Yep." Not only for this flight. All Kane owned— besides the business jet itself—could fit into two bags. He traveled light. And liked it that way.

"I appreciate your making the trip, son." Wearing faded jeans, a black turtleneck and down vest, Charlie looked younger than his fifty-six years, even with his salt-and-pepper hair.

"Just hold up your end of the deal, Dad."

"I will." Charlie picked up a box containing soda, water, ice, boxed lunches and a plate of cookies and brownies. "I will leave you alone. No more questions. No more badgering you to come home."

Home. That was a good one. Kane nearly laughed. There hadn't been a real home to come back to since his mom had died suddenly from a heart attack three years ago and his dad had quickly remarried...and divorced. Now his father looked poised to make the same mistake again.

"But—" Charlie pushed the box of food through the doorway of the cabin "—I still expect a card or e-mail or phone call at Christmastime."

"I can manage that." Easter and Father's Day, too. Even his dad's birthday. Kane would do anything to get away from Boston and never have to return. He didn't want to watch his father woo and wed yet another woman who could never take the place of his mother.

"Just remember, I love you, son. I'm here if you need me. For anything. Money, whatever."

Kane nodded once. He glanced at his watch. Damn. "Where is she?"

"Belle?" Charlie asked.

Kane fought the urge not to wince at his dad's newest "friend's" name. "The one I'm flying to Seattle."

"Serena will be here," Charlie said. "Traffic is always bad at this time."

Norwood Airport was twenty-five miles north of Boston. That meant she could be really late. Kane wanted to get in the air.

"Try smiling, son," Charlie said. "You might have fun. Serena James is a beautiful young woman."

"There are lots of beautiful women out there. No need to settle on just one."

Though a cross-country romance might not be too bad. As long as it was over by the time they returned home.

Charlie shook his head. "You just haven't met the right woman to love yet."

"I meet lots of women." Kane grinned. "Love them, too."

Charlie frowned. "I mean the forever kind of love. The kind I had with your mother."

And with his second wife.

And with what's-her-name. Belle.

Forever was a joke. And love—the kind his dad was talking about—was nothing more than a pretty word for convenient sex and companionship.

A white van pulled through the gate and honked its horn.

Charlie turned toward the sound. "They're here."

"Great." Kane had been hoping "they" would be a no-show.

A woman with silvery-blond hair and a beaming smile drove. She waved. Her passenger held a cell phone to her ear and wore dark, round sunglasses that hid much of her face.

The van stopped. The driver's door opened. The older woman, wearing brown pants and a colorful jacket, slid out gracefully.

"Good morning." She greeted Charlie with a handshake. The woman stepped toward Kane, extending her arm. "You must be Kane."

He shook her hand, noting her warmth and strong grip. She was different from his mother and his ex-stepmother. Older. Maybe even older than his father. That surprised Kane. "You must be Belle."

"I am." Her voice sounded like honey. Deep South honey. Slow and sweet. "I appreciate your flying Serena to Seattle."

Of course she did, especially with his father picking up all the associated flight and fuel costs.

"Kane's happy to do it," Charlie answered. "Aren't you, son?"

Kane nodded. He would be very happy once this trip was behind him and he'd be flying away for good.

"Well, we'd better get busy then." Belle opened the van doors and pulled out a box. "We have boxes to load. Brochures, favor samples and portfolios. Plus linens, flower arrangements, a cake and gowns."

Belle's eagerness to help surprised Kane. "O-kay."

"You still have to meet Serena James, our wedding dress designer," Belle said. "She's finishing up a phone call. No doubt talking to Rupert."

Kane bit. "Rupert?"

"Her boyfriend." Belle's ever present smile widened. "The two are practically engaged."

So much for a little romance in Seattle. Ring on the finger or not, Kane didn't mess around with another man's girl.

The passenger door opened. He focused on the woman exiting the van. She was, in a word, stunning. Long blond bangs fell over her forehead, but her hair didn't touch the collar of the jacket in the back. The short cut looked hip and trendy, just like the woman herself.

She wasn't tall, five-six if he was being generous and subtracted the heels on her brown leather boots. Even with her long wool coat, he could tell she had curves in all the right places.

He liked what he saw. She was exactly his type. Kane blew out a puff of breath that hung in the cold air. Old type, he corrected with a frown. He'd given up on blondes.

Her hair color coupled with the way she dressed re-minded him of a former girlfriend, Amber Wallersby, who had been sexy as hell, but also a spoiled, pampered princess. She'd wanted him to stop flying his grandfather around on his private jet and take a boring desk job at one of her father's companies so he could pamper her in the manner to which she'd become accustomed. Kane had almost agreed, almost been taken in, until he'd seen that she might have been gorgeous on the outside, but was all show and zero substance on the inside. `

Was Serena James the same?

Not that he was in any position to find out. Or care. Still they would be spending several hours flying west together. No sense starting off on the wrong foot.

"Hi," he said. "I'm your pilot. Kane."

Serena didn't extend her hand. She removed her sunglasses and glanced up at him. Clear, sharp eyes met his. He hadn't expected such directness or such stunning blue eyes.

"You're Kane Wiley?" Serena sounded surprised, almost as if she disapproved. "Charlie's son?"

"In the flesh."

"Do you see a family resemblance?" Charlie asked.

She glanced between the two men. "Not really."

"Oh, I do," Belle said. "Like father, like son. Both of you are quite handsome."

Charlie beamed.

Kane rocked back on his heels. He wasn't anything like his father. He didn't need a woman in his life—not on a permanent basis, anyway. And unlike his father, Kane's loyalty was hard to earn and his disapproval slow to fade.

"The eyes are the same," Serena conceded. "Maybe the chins, too."

The way she studied him made Kane uncomfortable. "We're running late. Let's get your stuff on board."

Serena glanced at Belle.

"Is something wrong, darlin'?" the woman asked. "Did you get a chance to say goodbye to Rupert?"

"Um, no."

Pink tinged Serena's cheeks.

Interesting. Kane wouldn't have thought her the blushing type. She seemed too cool and collected, but maybe leaving her "practically a fiancé" had rattled her.

"Would you mind if the gowns went in the cabin, Mr. Wiley?" she asked.

"It's Kane, and no, I don't mind."

The relief in her eyes was almost palpable. "I'll put them in the cabin."

"I'll load them."

"I don't mind doing it," she said.

"That's okay. I'd rather do it myself."

Serena eyed him warily. He waited for her to say something to challenge him. He was surprised when she didn't.

"You can put the food in the galley if you want," he offered. "It's in a box near the door."

"Fine."

Not fine if the tightness around her mouth was anything to go by. At least she didn't pout like Amber. Though he'd bet Serena could work wonders with that full bottom lip of hers.

As he removed several long, bulky white dress bags from the van, he heard his father.

"Kane prefers doing things on his own," Charlie explained.

"So does Serena," Belle added. "She likes being in control."

"Then the two of them should get along fine."

Nope, Kane realized. The exact opposite. Flying with

two captains in the cockpit was a recipe for disaster because neither wanted to give up control. And that meant one thing. It was going to be a really long flight to Seattle and back.

Serena had a checklist for her Mr. Right: polite, attentive, articulate, smartly tailored. All qualities her parents had taught her to value. All qualities Rupert had possessed in spades.

All qualities Kane Wiley lacked.

She unfastened her seat belt and moved back to where he'd secured the gowns.

What had Belle gotten her into?

Serena checked each of the dress bags. She repositioned three of them. Not much, but she felt better taking control. That is, taking care of her dresses. That was her job even if Kane didn't seem to realize that.

The man was arrogant and rude, the polar opposite of his kind and generous father, who epitomized a true gentleman. If not for the price of the flight—free, thanks to Charlie—and the ability to personally oversee the transport of the gowns, Serena would have found another way to Seattle. But any extra money The Wedding Belles had was going into a fund to pay for their cherished assistant, Julie's, wedding next June. They couldn't afford to be too choosy after losing money on the Vandiver cancellation and the negative publicity that had followed.

She thought about how much Julie and Matt were in love. Her other friends, too. Serena would find the same kind of love, the same kind of forever love, they had found. All she needed was her Mr. Right. One who didn't just look good on paper, but whom she could love, too.

Looking out of a window, she caught a glimpse of Kane

as he performed his preflight walk-around. Light glinted off his sun-streaked light brown hair that fell past the collar of his dark leather jacket. A jacket that emphasized his broad shoulders.

Talk about Mr. Wrong.

Some women might find him good-looking. If they liked tall, classically handsome guys with chiseled jawlines, square chins, sharpened noses and intense brown eyes.

Serena didn't object to any of those things, exactly. She just preferred them packaged in a suit and tie, and paired with a short, styled haircut and clean-shaven face. She didn't want a man who looked as if he'd rolled out of bed, bypassed the razor and brushed his fingers through his hair as an afterthought.

He glanced up at the plane, at the window she stared out of to be exact. His gaze met hers. His eyes, the same color of her favorite dark chocolate, made her heart bump.

Uh-oh.

She hurried back to her seat, sank into the comfortable leather club chair and fastened her seat belt. The temperature in the cabin seemed to rise even though the door was still open. She removed her coat, picked up her sketch pad and fanned herself.

What was the matter with her? Of course, she hadn't been sleeping well lately. Or eating, either. One good meal, and she'd feel better.

She'd like to take a bite out of Kane.

"Hot?"

Her sketch pad fell onto her lap. She looked up.

Kane stood at the entrance to the plane. The interior suddenly seemed smaller. He appeared larger. She gulped.

"Excuse me?" Serena asked.

"Are you hot?"

"I—I…" Something about him made her flustered and tongue-tied and heated. She didn't like the feelings, either. "I'm a little warm."

"I'll take care of it." He closed and latched the door. "Are your dresses okay?"

Serena heard the challenge in his voice. She raised her chin. "They are fine. Now."

The intensity in his dark eyes sent heat rushing through her veins. She sucked in a breath. Looked away.

"Seat belt fastened?" he asked.

Not trusting her voice, she nodded.

"The same rules apply on this flight as your typical commercial flight," Kane explained. "When we reach cruising altitude, you can visit the lavatory or help yourself to whatever you would like in the galley."

"No flight attendant?"

"Not unless you want to fly the plane while I serve you lunch and a beverage." He pointed out the exits and where the oxygen masks were located. "If we lose cabin pressure, place the mask over your nose and mouth and breath normally. Did you bring a laptop?"

"No." She'd wanted to escape from the constant pretending of her life in Boston. Her prying friends, her fake phone calls…even e-mail was a hassle these days. "Just my cell phone. I know not to use it during the flight."

"Even if you miss your boyfriend?"

She tried not to cringe, but the thought of lying to a total stranger left a bitter taste in her mouth. "It won't be a problem."

"Not using your cell phone or missing him?"

"Either."

At least that was the truth.

"If you need anything," he said, "let me know."

Serena could just imagine his reaction if she asked for, oh, a bag of pretzels and a fiancé. She bit back a smile.

No matter how desperately she wanted to maintain her image with her friends and family, she would never ask someone like Kane—someone so obviously wrong for a woman like her—to help in her quest to find a new Mr. Right and one true love.

That was something she could do on her own. And would.

CHAPTER TWO

"THE doors will open in ten minutes," announced a feminine voice over the convention center loudspeakers.

Ten minutes? Kane scanned the large hall, balancing the gold-wrapped box he'd promised to deliver to Serena. He'd thought he had more time.

Little-Miss-I'm-In-Charge Serena had sounded really upset when she'd called and asked if the box was still on the plane. When Kane had finally found the package in the tail-cone baggage compartment and brought it over, she'd told him she'd be right out. But he was already there, wasn't he?

And—admit it—he'd been curious to see the blonde in action. Curious enough to volunteer to deliver the box himself.

Man, was he sorry now. This wedding stuff gave him the heebie jeebies.

He might as well be standing in the middle of a wedding nightmare. Instead of fire, heat and screams, this place reeked with flowers, tulle and as much pipe organ music as the soundtrack of some cheesy Dracula movie.

A woman dressed in black with spiked red hair, flushed cheeks and a clipboard in her hand raced up to him. "Are you a fashion show model?"

"No."

"Where could they be?" Her face scrunched, then, as she studied him, brightened. "Would you want to be one of the models?"

Kane pictured himself dressed up like a penguin and escorting models in white dresses down a runway. He didn't mind models, but the other stuff... Not his thing. "No, thanks."

With a frustrated sigh, she ran down the aisle and disappeared out of sight.

She wasn't the only one in a hurry. Exhibitors rushed around, putting finishing touches on their booths and applying their lipstick. Kane didn't see many men, not like yesterday when he'd dropped off Serena to set up, but a few guys remained. This seemed like the last place any male would choose to spend an hour. Let alone a day. Or two.

Once, he might have thought about settling down someday, but now, after all he'd seen, Kane knew better.

As he searched the booths, every company seemed to have the word *wedding* somewhere in its name and everything looked sort of similar. He felt lost and out of place.

"Kane." He turned to see Serena waving at him. "Over here."

Relieved, he walked across the aisle to her booth. Whatever panic he'd heard in her voice wasn't visible on her face, looking fresh and rested with expertly applied makeup.

That's right, dummy, look at the lipstick. Keep your eyes on her face. She is so not your type.

But man, she looked good in that dress.

Her gaze was intent on him. "You made it."

"With minutes to spare."

"Minutes?" Serena asked.

"A few. Were you getting worried?"

Kane already knew the answer was yes. She seemed to keep a tight hold on her responsibilities, on pretty much everything within her sphere of influence. He happened to be the exact opposite, taking things as they came. It was probably a good thing she had an almost-fiancé. Because the way she looked, he could have been tempted into a fling. And the last thing he wanted or needed in his life was a cool blond control freak with a thing for weddings.

Serena took the box from him. "I wasn't worried, but I was getting a little impatient."

"Not the patient type?"

"Waiting for someone to come through can be hard."

"Sometimes."

But he wouldn't mind waiting right there. He didn't have to want to spend the rest of his life with her to enjoy the view. What man with blood running through his veins wouldn't want to look? Her brown and blue dress clung in all the right places. The hem fell above the knee, and her high heels made her legs look long and sexy. She defined "it" girl.

He didn't know whether to envy that Rupert fellow or pity him. Serena James was the type who knew how to make a guy roll over and beg. And Kane didn't sit, stay or play dead for any woman, no matter how hot she looked in heels.

"I do appreciate your bringing this over." She walked toward a linen-covered table with one of the elaborate floral arrangements she'd brought with her in the center. Candles in silver holders sat on either side. She tossed a smile his way. "Thank you."

Her gratitude sounded genuine. Kane couldn't tell

whether she was sincere or not, but he was willing to play nice. "You're welcome."

The gentle sway of her hips and the swirl of her dress hem around her legs captured his attention. The lingering scent of her light floral perfume filled his nostrils.

Serena opened the box. "Now all I have to do is set these things out and the table will be ready."

The table already looked finished and fancy enough to him. A little too fancy, but probably what the monkey-suit, bouquet-tossing set expected. "What's in there?"

"Chocolate." As she unwrapped each item, she placed the pieces of candy on an oval beveled-edged mirror setting on the table: three chocolate truffles shaped like three-tiered wedding cakes, small gold and silver boxes tied with ribbon, oval and heart-shaped engraved chocolates packaged in a gold base and wrapped with tulle and a ribbon, gold and silver engraved foiled coins. "No wedding is complete without something chocolate."

"I don't care much for weddings, but I like chocolate."

Her eyebrows rose at his not-so-subtle hint, but she tossed a coin his way.

He unwrapped the gold foil and took a bite. Good stuff. "Aren't you having any?"

"I don't sample the merchandise," she said in her cool, controlled voice.

Yeah. Right. Probably one of those salad-and-rice-cake types who wouldn't let herself eat a piece of candy. Too bad. She had a sweet little body, but he'd rather see a woman enjoy a meal with dessert than starve in order to fit into a smaller size.

She hid the box underneath the linen tablecloth–covered round table displaying a four-tiered white-iced wedding cake decorated with real flowers cascading down from the top like a colorful pink and white waterfall. "All done."

He'd say so. Judging by this booth, The Wedding Belles was a high-class, high-end operation. From the neatly stacked full-color brochures to the maroon leather embossed photo albums, everything shouted "money." Including Serena herself.

Kane leisurely finished his chocolate, surveying the booth. He noticed a stack of boxes. Board games, actually. Who would have thought to make a game out of getting married? Playing that sounded more like torture than fun.

A burgundy upholstered chaise longue sat at a right angle to a row of headless mannequins in white—the Wedding Shop of Horrors. "Looks like someone went furniture shopping last night."

"We contracted with a rental store here in Seattle who delivered all this yesterday."

"You must have worked all night."

She pushed a strand of hair back from her face. "Just doing my job."

"Don't you design the wedding dresses?"

"Each of us helps out where we can," she said. "That's why working for The Wedding Belles is such fun."

Fun? Serena never seemed to stop working. She moved through the booth adjusting swags of rich yellow fabric draped on the boring white panels separating each of the exhibit areas.

Didn't she ever slow down or rest? Even sitting on the flight she'd been working on something. He didn't know how she did it.

"Everything looks good," he said.

"Good won't cut it. Brides are the pickiest people on

this planet, next to their mothers." She straightened a stack of brochures. "Everything needs to be perfect."

"Nothing's ever perfect."

"Then you've never attended a wedding put on by The Wedding Belles." Kneeling, she realigned the hem of one of the wedding dresses. "Or worn one of my gowns."

"No offense, but I don't look my best in a train and heels."

She smiled up at him.

He smiled back.

Now this was more like it.

"Do you need anything?" he asked. "Breakfast? Coffee?"

Me.

"Thanks, but I already ate and my coffee is stashed where I can get to it easily." Standing, she peeked at her watch. "You might want to get going. The doors are going to—"

"Welcome to the Northwest Fall Bridal Extravaganza," the voice over the loudspeaker announced.

"Uh-oh. You didn't make it out in time. Watch out." Serena smoothed the skirt of her dress. "We're about to be overrun by the bridal brigade commanded by mothers and supported by best friends, sisters and cousins."

Within seconds, chattering, laughter and even shrieks filled the large hall as if someone had turned off the mute switch on the remote. Packs of women ran past him.

"Where are they going?" he asked.

"The first fashion show."

Had he agreed to model, all those women would have been running to him. Wonder what Blondie would say to that? A smile tugged on his lips.

Two young women walked up to her with questions about the cake on display.

The once empty aisles and booths were now crowded with women lugging ten-pound bags of bridal literature. Lots of women. Young ones, old ones…mostly young ones. Good-looking, too.

And engaged, Kane reminded himself. He didn't do engaged women. Or even almost-engaged women, like Serena.

"Mom." A twenty-something woman with chestnut hair wearing a green baby-doll style dress rushed into The Wedding Belles' booth. "This is it. I have to have this dress."

"We've been here two minutes and that's the third dress you've said that about," the mother said.

"Mo-om."

Serena was speaking to two other women, but that didn't stop the mother from interrupting the conversation.

"How much is this wedding gown?" the mother asked.

"I'm sorry, but that dress is not for sale," Serena explained. "It will be worn at a wedding on November 22."

The daughter's collagen-injected, shimmery pink lips puckered like some kind of bizarre human-hybrid fish. Kane grinned to himself. Maybe this was the Northwest version of bridezilla.

"Could you make one like this for my daughter?" the mother asked, not-so-subtly showing off her designer purse and iceberg-sized diamond ring.

Despite the interruptions, Serena smiled pleasantly. "I can create something just as beautiful for her. With your daughter's lovely figure, an asymmetrical A-line gown would be stunning. A cutaway skirt, even. And champagne embroidered lace would be a wonderful accent with her coloring."

The bride tossed her artfully streaked hair. "We'd pay you extra for that dress on display."

Kane would have told the mother to take her money and... Well, go someplace else.

"If you are interested in our gowns, we have a couple of samples here that can be sold off-the-rack." Serena's smile never wavered as she motioned to the photo albums on the table. "You might also want to make yourself comfortable and glance through the portfolio to get a taste of all our designs."

"We might come back later." The mother looked down her surgically designed pert nose. "Or not."

The words didn't seem to faze Serena. "I'll be here."

The way she handled herself with the appearances-are-everything, I-can-buy-whatever-I-want attitude impressed Kane. He only hoped she wasn't cut from the same cloth. Not that it meant anything to him if she were.

As the bride stomped away, more women fawned over the dresses. Serena answered their questions not only promoting her gowns, but the services provided by The Wedding Belles, especially when it came to full-service destination weddings.

She was in her element. Glowing, sparkling, radiant.

Kane slowly backed away. He liked watching her, but this wasn't the place for a single guy intent on remaining that way.

Serena gave a quick nod his way. He was surprised she'd noticed him leaving. He was also surprised he liked her noticing.

Uh-oh. Not good. Very bad actually.

Serena James might not have a ring on her finger, but

avoiding her was the smart thing to do. The right thing to do, even if he spent another night in his hotel room alone watching television. On second thought, maybe he could find a bridesmaid, sprinkled among the brides and their mothers, here with something on her mind besides marriage.

Maybe all the shiny fabrics and chocolate would put her in the mood for satin sheets and room service. And maybe that would get his mind off a certain "practically engaged" someone.

He glanced back at Serena.

Or…maybe not.

"Thanks for dinner, Malcolm." Malcolm Rapier was Serena's friend and former classmate from design school. She kissed his cheek, expertly avoiding his twist to meet her mouth. "It was great catching up with you."

"Sure you don't want to go to the party?" With his boyish grin, he looked more like one of his models than the rising star of men's formal wear design. "I'd love to show you off."

Serena was tempted. Talk about a looker in a stylish black suit he'd designed himself and multicolored silk tie. Almost as handsome as Kane. Where had that come from?

"I usually enjoy being shown off, but I didn't sleep much last night." Going out wasn't a good idea when she wanted to yawn. Not to mention her feet ached.

"Understood. Return of bridezilla tomorrow." He laced his fingers with hers, his hands warm and smooth like the fabrics he dealt with every day. "But if you change your mind, call me. I'll send the limo back."

"You're too sweet."

Unlike her pilot. *The* pilot, she corrected.

"No, you're too sexy and look great on my arm." Malcolm twirled her to him as if they were dancing and pulled her against him. "Any chance you'd leave Boston for Seattle?"

Serena knew exactly how the game was played... Normally she would concede, but she didn't like the way Kane kept intruding on her thoughts. She wanted to prove to herself the pilot had no effect on her.

She looked up at Malcolm through her eyelashes. "Why would I want to do that?"

"Oh, Serena, my muse, can't you imagine the beautiful formal wear we could create together? Paris, Milan, New York. Nothing could compete with us."

"You're right about that." But Serena wanted more than that kind of partnership. She wanted true love—marriage and children. She eyed Malcolm subjectively, as if inventorying the pieces of her next design. "Would this be strictly a business arrangement?"

He lowered his mouth to her ear, his warm breath tickling her skin. "Do you think I'd ask you to relocate across the country just for a job?"

Maybe she was going a little too far here. Okay, Malcolm and she would make a stunning pair. They shared common interests and enjoyed each other's company. Yet if she were at all interested in pursuing a relationship with him, why couldn't she get Kane out of her mind?

His smile widened. "You're thinking about it."

Not really. At least not with him. She shrugged.

"You are." Laughing, Malcolm caressed her cheek with his fingertip and kissed her forehead. "Until tomorrow, my soon-to-be Seattle love and partner."

With that he walked out of the revolving door to hit whatever hip parties were happening that night. She wasn't sad to see him go.

Serena's heels clicked on the marble floor of the hotel lobby. Even after the long day at the bridal show, she felt reenergized though her body's internal clock was running three hours ahead.

The first day of the Northwest Bridal Extravaganza had been a hit, an "in the park home run" to quote one of the Seattle show's organizers. Tomorrow might just be a grand slam. Serena already felt like an all-star.

"What would Rupert say?"

She recognized the voice and stopped, annoyed that Kane had not only been on her mind, but was now here. He sat at a nearby table with a pint of beer in his hand, looking totally comfortable and at ease. In his jeans and long-sleeved black T-shirt, he had that carefree, I-don't-care-what-you-think, sexy style down. Not that she thought he was sexy. Her type of sexy, that was.

Oh, she'd once been tempted by bad boys, but her sister's experience had made Serena immune to their charms. Her sister, Morgan, had fallen in love with a guy who'd had women calling him day and night. He had no steady job nor seemed to want one. Morgan had moved in with him anyway and then married him, claiming he loved her and would change. He hadn't and didn't. Serena had been the one to pick up the pieces when his infidelity destroyed the marriage and left her pregnant sister devastated and alone. Their parents still hadn't forgiven Morgan for falling in love with the wrong man and "ruining" her life.

"What do you mean by that?" Serena asked.

He motioned to an empty seat.

She really shouldn't.

She really wanted to.

Kane pushed the chair out from the small round table with his foot. "You can buy me a drink for this morning."

Her mouth curved. "You already have one."

"I wouldn't mind another."

She did owe him for dropping off the box on time, even if he had waited until the last possible minute. She sat, grateful the moment her bottom hit the leather chair and she was no longer standing.

"Oooh," she moaned.

His brows lifted. "You're easily satisfied."

She flushed. "I should look into designing a high heel that could be worn for fourteen hours straight without causing foot pain."

"I meant the guy. For a woman who's practically engaged, you seemed pretty chummy with Mr. Suit."

Each time Serena heard that phrase—practically engaged—she felt as if another heavy bolt of fabric had been stapled to her shoulders. And right now she didn't like the judgmental tone of Kane's voice. He didn't know her. He knew nothing about her. "Are you a pilot or a chaperone?"

"Pilot. Unattached. But if you were my girl—" his gaze traveled over her with lazy appreciation "—I sure wouldn't want you having dinner or cozying up with another man."

Tingles shot through her and she sat straighter. Her reaction had everything to do with being tired and nothing to do with him. "Then it's a good thing I'm not your girl, isn't it?"

"A damn good thing."

Serena winced. She wasn't used to such rudeness or honesty. She didn't know what to say. That left her more than a little flustered. She could always be counted on to find the right words or do the right thing.

"Let me guess," he continued. "Your boyfriend is a carbon copy of the guy you were with."

"Malcolm Rapier is the guy's name, and he's a little like

Rupert." Only better. Malcolm was a better dresser than her ex. "He's a fellow designer and a friend."

"Who wants to be more than a friend."

It wasn't a question. "And you know this because…"

"I'm a guy."

"And guys know everything."

"You said it." Kane raised his glass.

"Malcolm likes pretty things," she said.

Kane took a swig of beer. "Things?"

"Women." She didn't know why she was wasting her time explaining things to him. "Malcolm likes to be seen escorting attractive women around. You know, arm candy."

Which was probably why he wanted her to move to Seattle. A built-in date to take to social functions. Not exactly the strongest foundation for a lasting relationship.

Kane's mouth quirked. "Modest, aren't we?"

"You asked."

"I did." A beat passed. "So Rupert—"

"Doesn't worry." The words tumbled from her lips. Not exactly a lie. Her ex-boyfriend didn't care what she did. "There's no need."

"You're a one-woman man."

"Yes, I am." When she had a man. "I've never understood people who play the field."

"As long as the individuals involved know what's going on, I don't see a problem with it."

"That's because you're a guy."

"Women play the field, too," Kane said. "Otherwise, it would get mighty lonely out there."

"Were you lonely tonight?" she asked.

"No." He swirled his glass. "I had dinner with a lovely bridesmaid who had only one thing on her mind."

"What was that?"

"Becoming a bride."

Serena laughed. "You don't want to get married?"

"Nope," he said. "Marital bliss isn't for me."

She wasn't surprised. He didn't look like husband or daddy material. But if a woman were looking for a temporary lover instead of something more permanent...

"What *do* you want?" Serena asked, curious.

He got a faraway look in his eyes. "Freedom."

She'd never known freedom in her entire life. She was always working toward something, fulfilling an obligation or meeting a responsibility. "I'm sure that must be nice."

"You should try it sometime."

Temptation sparked. And then she thought about her parents. She couldn't do anything to upset them. "Not my style."

"Mr. Suit is your style?" Kane asked.

"Pretty much."

"Too bad."

"Not for Mr. Suit."

He nodded then stopped. "Except for Rupert."

"Ah, yes. Rupert."

"Women like you need to open your eyes," Kane said. "The perfect guy could be right in front of you, but if he wasn't your 'style' you'd walk right by and miss your chance."

"Love will find a way."

Kane studied her. "You really buy into all this wedding stuff, don't you?"

"Completely," she said.

"Well, then." He raised his glass to her. "I'm sure you'll find exactly what you're looking for."

"You, too," she said. "A juicy piece of eye candy like yourself must have women falling at your feet."

"Pretty much."

A smile erupted across Kane's face. The effect—devastatingly charming. Serena moistened her lips, trying not to stare.

"Juicy, huh? Thanks." He placed his empty glass on the table. "It's not often I get a compliment from an esteemed piece of arm candy."

"It's not often I give them." Uh-oh. She was flirting. But she kind of liked how it felt. "Do you want that drink now?"

"I'll take a rain check."

A twinge of disappointment ran through her. Ridiculous.

Serena was just having a little fun. Nothing more. She knew what she wanted to find. It sure wasn't Kane Wiley.

CHAPTER THREE

THE next afternoon, Kane eyed the altocumulus clouds to the west. No immediate danger there. The weather service had issued an icing advisory at high altitudes, but they'd be flying below the problem. His plane was only certified to forty-five thousand feet. Still he wanted to get in the air.

As soon as his passenger got off her damn pink cell phone.

"Yes, Belle," Serena said. "Both the local paper and the magazine took photos."

"Hang up," Kane ordered. "Time to go."

Serena held up a single, slim finger in response: One minute.

He'd already given up more than a minute.

Back at the convention center, photographers had swarmed The Wedding Belles' booth, snapping pictures and jotting down quotes from Serena. She really was some kind of hotshot in the wedding world.

Kane had suffered the commotion as well and as long as he could. He could see success was important to her. Anyway, his dad was paying for his time. Complaining wasn't going to get him anything but a headache.

But after the Suit had shown up, eager to shower Serena

with congratulations and kisses and who knew what else, Kane's patience had evaporated. He wasn't a clocks-and-schedules kind of guy, but the weather system pushing down from Canada wasn't waiting while Serena played kissy-face with her designer buddy.

Now Kane was waiting again. The plane had been fueled. He had loaded their food and luggage, filed his flight plan and completed his walk-around. It was time—past time—to go.

"Get in the plane."

She raised her index finger again, like a dog trainer hushing a barking pooch.

Kane bit back a growl and grabbed her phone.

"She's got to go," he said into the tiny receiver. "She'll call you later."

He switched off the phone and tossed it into the plane, onto her seat.

"What did you do that for?" Lines creased Serena's forehead. "I was only on the phone for a couple of min-utes."

"Try twenty," he corrected.

Serena opened her mouth then pressed her lips together. She entered the plane. He followed her.

"A couple storms are brewing with a low pressure system off the Pacific." Kane locked the door. "There's weather in Canada that's moving south."

"Why didn't you tell me?" she asked.

"You were on the phone."

Serena removed her coat. Took her a pad out of her bag. Sat down.

Kane recognized the silent treatment. The way her eyes avoided his. Amber used to do that. So did a lot of other women. He wouldn't let Serena make him feel guilty. Not when *she* should be apologizing to *him*.

"The weather shouldn't affect us," he said. "But keep your seat belt fastened in case we hit any turbulence."

She buckled herself up. "Not a problem."

"There's food in the galley, but be quick about it because of the—"

"Turbulence," she finished for him. "I will, and, Kane…"

"Yeah."

"I'm sorry for taking so long." Her gaze captured his, her big blue eyes apologetic. Appealing. Not like Amber at all. Not like any other of the women in his life. "I know you delayed our departure back at the convention center, and I really appreciate that, but I was excited. I wanted to share the news of all the good publicity and photo ops with my friends."

He grunted. "No worries."

Kane lied.

He was worried plenty. Not about the weather. He was a good pilot. Surface wind speeds were acceptably low, and the system coming in was moving slowly enough that it shouldn't be a problem.

His reaction to her, however, was a whole other story.

Kane was upset at her. Serena stared out the small window at the overcast sky.

Even though he'd accepted her apology, she could tell he didn't like being made to wait. She didn't like waiting, either. Time to make it up to him?

Not necessary, a voice in her head whispered.

He'd been a jerk.

He'd grabbed her phone.

He'd hung up on Belle.

Kane had explained all that. She could forgive his impatience to get in the air. She wasn't quite as ready to let go of his brusque rejection last night.

Then it's a good thing I'm not your girl, isn't it?

A damn good thing.

Serena bit her lip. Kane hadn't even let her buy him a beer. He'd wanted a "rain check."

Not that she cared. Not much anyway.

Unless his wanting a "rain check" was his way of seeing her in Boston. Maybe it was time to find out.

They hadn't hit any turbulence. Now that they were at cruising altitude, Serena unfastened her seat belt and went to the galley that reminded her more of a refreshment center than an actual kitchen. Still the efficiently designed space made it easy to pour a cup of coffee, find two freshly baked cookies and put them on a napkin. She carried everything to the cockpit.

Payback? Or peace offering?

Either way, she didn't want to owe Kane anything.

"I brought you a snack," she said.

He glanced back. "What?"

"Coffee and chocolate-chip cookies." He liked chocolate, she remembered. "I, um, owe you a drink, remember? There wasn't any cream—"

"Black is fine." He took the food from her. "Thanks."

Okay, she was done now. "I'll be going back."

"Come on up," he said at the same time.

Kane motioned to the other seat. "Sit up here for a while."

Serena stared at the high-tech-looking instrument panel with a small computerlike device between the two pilot seats. Not a lot of space up here.

She glanced at the cabin. Safer, back there.

"Plenty of room," Kane said. "This baby's simple enough for one pilot, but it can be flown by two."

"I can't fly."

His attractive mouth curved. "But you can sit, right?"

She crawled into the seat and peered out the window. The one-hundred-and-eighty-degree view took her breath away. Clouds blanketed the sky as far as she could see. She couldn't tell where the ground was or where the sky ended. Forget about locating the horizon. "Wow."

The word described how she felt inside. Every nerve ending tingled. Her insides buzzed.

Being up here, cocooned in the small cockpit with Kane and cut off from the earth below, made all her problems seem a world away. A world she wasn't in any hurry to return to.

"Fasten your seat belt," he said.

The harness-style seat belt went over her shoulders and around her waist. She had trouble buckling it. Kane reached over to help her. The warm skin of his hands brushed hers, sending tiny shocks down to the tips of her fingers.

Nothing. It meant nothing. "I've got it."

"Sure?" he asked.

She wasn't sure about anything. Still she nodded and clipped the buckle in.

"Most of the weather is behind us," he said. "It should be smooth flying. We might even make up some time."

"Good."

But it wasn't. Not really.

Serena wasn't ready to return to Boston. She wanted this time, a time with no lies, no expectations to uphold and no responsibility a little while longer. The bridal show in Seattle had been stressful, but also successful. Coming off that high, she was still literally flying, and she'd never felt such freedom as she did now.

Was that what Kane liked? The freedom? The ability to go wherever he wanted, whenever he wanted? She could definitely understand that appeal now.

She glanced his way. "So…do you like to fly?"

He gave her a look.

Okay, dumb question.

Serena would try again. "How long have you been flying?"

"Since I was sixteen. It's the only thing I've ever wanted to do."

"Why did you choose to be a charter pilot and not an airline pilot?"

"I thought about doing the corporate gig, but it's too much like working for a bus company. My grandfather bought a business jet. When he offered me a job as his personal pilot, I jumped at it. I flew for him for six years, until he got sick." Kane's mouth tightened. "He doesn't travel anymore."

Her chest tightened. "I'm sorry."

"Why? I got my hands on this plane for next to nothing and my grandfather's instructions were to make my own way in the wild blue yonder. That's what I've been doing."

Serena envied his go-where-the-wind-carried-him attitude. She'd planned out her entire life. Rarely did she go out to eat without reservations.

"How often do you fly?" she asked, wanting to learn more about him. Something about Kane Wiley intrigued her in a way she'd never felt before.

"All the time." He patted the yoke. "This baby isn't only how I make my living. It's where I call home."

"Home." She thought about her painstakingly decorated flat in Boston. "You and me. We're very different."

"Nothing wrong with that."

Serena nodded.

He was rootless, a wanderer, free. She was tied down by her business, responsibility, expectations.

But at this moment, for as long as it could last, Serena wanted to enjoy the flight and this time with Kane, in spite of their differences and because of them. She wanted a taste—a nibble really—of what his life was like.

"You're such a free spirit," she said.

"I like to go where I want to go."

"And Boston?"

"A layover," he said. "Nothing more."

"Isn't your family there?"

"My dad." Kane pushed a couple of buttons. "We don't always see eye to eye on things."

"My sister is like that with my mom and dad. That's made things…difficult."

For all of them.

"What about you and your parents?" he asked.

"I get along fine with my folks."

She'd made sure of that.

"Lucky."

Serena nodded. But feeling lucky had nothing to do with her parents and everything to do with the sexy man sitting next to her. She held back a sigh.

A button lit up on the instrument panel. Kane immediately noticed it. Sat straighter. Furrowed his brow.

Her heart jolted. "Is something wrong?"

"Nope, but I need to take care of that light." He studied the instrument panel. "Would you mind going back to the cabin and fastening your seat belt?"

"Sure." She unbuckled the harness and squeezed out of the seat. "I'll see you later."

He nodded, pulling out some kind of manual.

Serena returned to her seat and buckled her seat belt. Leaning back, she blew out a puff of air.

What had she been thinking? Doing up there?

That warning light had been a sign, a reminder that she was better off earthbound. She needed to get her head out of the clouds. Being up in the air was a dangerous place. And being with Kane...

She didn't want any turbulence in her well-planned life.

Why was engine number two's damn fuel filter light on?

Kane stared on the instrument panel. He reset the circuit. The light remained on.

Interesting.

He had dealt with this before and knew what to do, but with Serena on board, he glanced at the flight procedure's manual to make sure he hadn't forgotten anything.

Okay. Just as he remembered. One fuel filter light. No problem. He would wait and see what happened next.

The usual chatter filled the radio airwaves. Nothing to worry about.

Kane focused his attention on the instrument panel. Everything was looking good.

The other fuel filter light popped on.

His stomach knotted in about a hundred different ways.

Two fuel filter lights meant fuel contamination. Damn. The plane had been filled with bad gas.

Kane took a deep breath and exhaled.

Okay, he'd trained for this. He knew what to do.

As he ran through emergency procedures in his head,

he flipped to the appropriate section of the flight manual and began the checklist.

Kane radioed his situation to the flight center and was cleared for descent. The only problem would be finding a place to land in the middle of nowhere. If worst came to worst, he could always set down on a freeway or road. Other pilots had done it.

At least the weather was holding. Though the sky had darkened above him. All he needed was clear weather to land this baby. Then the skies could open up with rain, snow, sleet or all of the above.

He thought about Serena sitting in the back by herself. She would be safer back there. Still he needed to prepare her for what might happen.

As the altimeter spun to a lower altitude, Kane searched for a landing spot. All he saw were mountains, trees and canyons. Lots of snow. Not good.

Over the years he'd had a couple of minor incidents in the air and an aborted takeoff, but nothing like this and never with a passenger on board. A big-eyed blonde who looked out of the cockpit like she was tasting freedom for the first time.

Sweat ran down his back and slicked his grip on the controls. Kane flipped on the intercom.

"Listen, Serena," he announced, his voice calm and steady. "You need to prepare for an emergency landing. All items need to be stored securely. That includes the galley. Once you're done, check your seat belt. Make sure it's flat and tight across your lower torso. When I say 'brace,' I want you to keep your feet flat on the floor and bend forward so you're facing down at your lap. Hold on to your ankles or legs. It might be a little bumpy, but everything will be okay."

As long as he could set down before the engines stopped turning, everything would be okay.

Unfortunately with bad fuel, Kane had no idea how long the engines would keep working.

Emergency landing?

Every one of Serena's muscles tensed.

Okay, that explained why they were descending. She glanced out of the window at the tree-covered, snowcapped mountains. Where were they? Washington? Oregon? Maybe even Idaho?

She didn't understand what was going on. She didn't like not knowing.

Except for that light, everything seemed fine. Nothing out of the ordinary, except for an edge to Kane's otherwise calm voice. Something she hadn't heard before.

Worst-case scenarios filled her mind. She tapped her feet. Flexed her fingers. Imagined dying.

Don't think about it. Stay in control. Do what Kane told you.

With a plan of action in place, Serena reached for her sketch pad and pencil. With trembling hands, she shoved them into her bag and placed it under a seat. Next she checked the galley and then her dresses. Everything seemed okay. Secure. Nothing should fly around if they had a rough landing.

Her heart pounded.

She hoped that was all it was.

Focusing on slow, even breaths, Serena sat and tightened her seat belt. She double-checked it, giving the strap one last tug.

Despite that tantalizing interlude in the cockpit, she knew this trip with Tall, Dark and Sexy had been a mistake.

She shivered. She should have stayed firmly on the ground in Boston, where she belonged. Freedom, even a taste of it, wasn't for her. Whether something was wrong with the plane or not, it was too…dangerous.

A strange, whining noise sounded, as if something was winding down. She thought about covering her ears, but clasped the armrests instead, gripping them so hard her knuckles turned white. An image of Kane, so confident and sure, flying the plane popped into her head making her feel safer, calmer.

Suddenly everything went quiet. Too quiet. Her breath rasped in the silence.

Oh, no.

Realization struck, chilling her to the bone. The engines had stopped. Her jaw clenched. She stared out of the window.

The mountains, so beautiful only moments ago, now loomed dark and deadly below. They seemed closer. The trees taller.

Her heart slammed against her chest.

The plane soared down through the sky, silent as a balsam-wood glider.

Fear and panic rioted through her.

Emergency landing? Not crash landing.

Right now Serena wasn't sure of anything. She hated the feeling. The lack of control. The whim of fate.

Tears stung her eyes. She'd planned her entire life out, what she wanted and when, but all of her plans didn't seem worth much now.

Serena thought about her family and friends. She swallowed around the lump in her throat. She wanted to tell them how much she loved them. She wanted…a second chance.

"Brace," Kane shouted.

Her heart pounding in her ears, she bent over and grabbed on to her ankles.

Please let it be over quickly, she prayed.

For a moment nothing happened. The quiet seemed...unnatural.

Then the plane slammed into the ground. The impact sent her forward against the seat belt. Knocked the wind out of her. Jostled her around.

Something hit her in the head.

Serena ignored the ache in her stomach, the pain from her head, the sticky, oozing substance rolling down the side of her face. She concentrated on holding on to her ankles. And breathing. It hurt to breathe.

Kane yelled something. Was he okay? She struggled for a breath. Yelling was out of the question.

The plane bounced like a ball. Metal shrieked and rattled. The sounds, worse than the crunching of two cars in an accident, made her want to cover her ears, but she couldn't let go of her legs.

How much longer?

Make it stop, Kane.

The plane veered, skidded to the right. Serena squeezed her eyes closed and screamed.

CHAPTER FOUR

SERENA'S scream shivered through the cockpit.

Kane broke into a cold sweat.

He gripped the yoke, his muscles straining to regain control of the speeding plane. The plane jostled, skidding and bouncing on the deceptively flat snow. He couldn't worry about what lay hidden underneath that white blanket. A row of trees loomed straight ahead. He stepped harder on the brakes.

Come on, baby. Stop for Papa.

The lights on the control panel flickered. What the...? No engines, no electricity, no control.

And Serena, along for the ride.

Kane swore, wrestling the unresponsive yoke as the forest hurtled closer. Individual trees sprang out of the shadowed mass. Far too little space between the solid trunks. Heavy, snow-laden branches. Sharp, frozen pine needles.

Fear was flat and bitter in his mouth.

A hard jolt knocked Kane to the right. He yelled a single word of warning. "Serena!" His harness held in place. The plane veered, dipped, rolled. The teeth-clenching squeal of tearing metal knotted his stomach.

Time slowed.

Falling sideward, Kane clutched the yoke, his knuckles white, his heart lodged in his throat. The flight manual flew across the cockpit, impacting the window with a loud boom. He expected to be next, but the harness straps dug into his skin, keeping him secured against his seat.

The plane spun, skidding on its side, away from the trees, and slowly, ever so slowly, came to a stop.

"Serena?"

A question now. A prayer. A plea.

His already pounding heart slammed against his chest. He unbuckled his harness, dropping hard against the center console. He lurched toward the cabin, stumbling over cabinets that now made up the floor. Nothing was where it should be. Light streamed in from the windows above him. Cold air seeped inside from a gash in the fuselage.

Had the tanks ruptured? Was the fuselage or wing on fire?

His breath steamed in the freezing draft. "Serena?"

"Here."

Her soft voice brought a rush of relief. She drooped at an awkward angle still strapped to her seat. One side of her face was covered in blood. She clutched her stomach.

But she was breathing. Responsive. And unless she'd broken her neck, he had to move her before the plane caught fire. Or started sliding again into the trees.

Ripping off the bottom of his shirt, he pressed the wadded material to her bleeding scalp. She gasped in protest.

"Where does it hurt?"

"My head and stomach. Ribs, I think." Her voice sounded strained, almost breathless. "Not bad."

Bad enough. "We need to get off the plane. Can you move?"

"I… Yes."

Her quiet voice bothered him, but he had to get her away from the plane in case of a fuel leak and/or fire. "Good. I'll help you."

Kane reached across her. His forearm brushed her stomach.

She winced.

"Sorry." Worry made him brusque.

"It's okay."

Kane released the buckle. "Let's go."

She glanced to the back of the cabin. "The wedding dresses."

"There isn't time, Serena." Kane opened the door and stepped out. His feet sunk six inches through a crusty layer of snow. No way did he want Serena wading through this.

"This might hurt." He placed one arm around her back and the other under her knees. As he lifted her from the plane, she inhaled sharply.

"Don't apologize," she said.

"I wasn't going to." He carried her from the plane, ignoring the soft curves pressing against him, until he felt they were far enough away in case of an explosion. "Can you stand?"

"Yes."

She didn't sound too certain. Carefully, he placed her on her feet, not letting go until he was certain she wouldn't fall or faint.

"I'm fine." Serena crossed her arms in front of her. "Really."

He took a long look at her. No coat, bleeding head,

arms around possibly injured ribs. "You sure have a different definition of 'fine' than I do."

Her gaze dropped.

Damn. That wasn't the reaction he wanted. He wanted to rouse her, to make her fighting mad. She would need all the fight in her, all her determination and vitality and assurance, to survive this.

"I'll bring back your coat and blankets," he said. "Stay here. I've got to check the plane for any fuel leaks."

Holding the cloth against her head, Serena nodded gingerly.

His breath hung in the crisp, pine-scented air. He lingered, oddly reluctant to leave her. "I'll be right back."

She made a shooing motion with the hand protecting her ribs. "Go."

He did.

A quick but thorough walk-around showed no fuel leaks. Kane checked both engines and the aircraft itself.

The plane lay on its side, crippled and crumpled and torn. Had the landing gear broken and caused the plane to roll? With all these trees in the meadow he wouldn't be surprised if they'd hit something. Whatever the reason, the sight in front of him broke his heart.

Everything he had—his livelihood, his home, his love— was gone. Just like that. Just like his mother. He set his jaw.

His life hadn't flashed before his eyes in the damn crash. But now Kane saw her, his mother, lying again on the floor of the kitchen. He'd heard a crash, run downstairs and found her. Unconscious. Her right hand on her heart. A broken bowl of bread dough next to her. He'd checked her breathing. None. Her pulse. None. But that hadn't stopped him from calling for help, applying the first aid measures he'd learned over the years, but nothing he did, nothing he tried, could disguise the fact it was too late to save her.

Just like it was too late to save the plane.

Kane shook himself. He still needed supplies, blankets. Serena needed blankets. He crawled into the plane.

First stop—the ELT, emergency locator transmitter. Not working. Kane tried the radio. Nothing. Not even static.

This wasn't looking good.

Sure, he'd radioed his final coordinates, but the plane had drifted several miles while he searched for a safe place to land. The search would start from the last known coordinates and spread out from there. Even if the weather held off, that could mean a long wait before they were found. Especially with this meadow that wasn't really big enough to land a plane. They were lucky. Damn lucky.

They were also missing. Lost. Screwed.

At least he didn't smell fuel.

They could stay inside the plane until they were rescued. Although that tear in the fuselage meant they were in for a long, cold night. He'd have to fix that, somehow, in the remaining daylight.

Kane scoured the cockpit and cabin, salvaging a first aid kit, flashlight, lighter, food, water, blankets, pillows and toilet paper from where they'd been tossed and tumbled around the aircraft. He found Serena's purse secured cleverly to the bottom of her seat, and then—finally!—her long wool coat, buried beneath another seat. Clutching it and a blanket, he trudged through the snow, returning to the exact spot where he'd left Serena.

Only…she wasn't there.

He gripped her coat and the blanket, looked around. Panic hollowed his gut. "Serena."

A million and one thoughts screamed through his brain.

Idiot.

He shouldn't have left her alone out here. She had a head injury. Possibly fractured or bruised ribs. Shock. Even the onset of hypothermia.

She couldn't have disappeared on a snow-covered meadow somewhere in middle-of-nowhere Idaho. He noticed a trail of footprints in the snow.

Anger slightly eclipsed his worry.

She could, however, have wandered off.

"Serena?" Kane called her name as he followed her trail to the edge of the meadow where a hillside—more like a mountain—rose up steeply.

No way would she climb up there. In her condition. In high-heeled boots.

But the footprints led upward. Was she disoriented? Confused? A concussion, maybe.

Or maybe she was just plain dumb.

He climbed up after her.

"Serena?" No answer. He hadn't been gone that long. Five minutes. Tops. She couldn't have climbed too high. Unless she'd passed out. His chest tightened. "Serena?"

"I'm right here." Her low voice sounded almost husky. She carefully made her way down the slope, teetering on her heels in the snow.

He climbed to meet her. Relief at finding her didn't appease his anger. Her face was white, her lips nearly blue.

"What the hell were you doing?" His already skyrocketing blood pressure spiked higher. "I told you to stay put not walk into a forest. You could have gotten lost or hurt or—"

"I was trying to get a signal on my cell phone." She pulled the thin, hot-pink device out of her pocket, her hands shaking. He was shaking, too, with reaction. "I wanted to call 911."

As if the local fire department could be here in three minutes to help them out of this situation. Kane bundled Serena roughly into her coat and wrapped the blanket over her, hoping she wouldn't notice his trembling hands. "And what if you couldn't find your way back?"

"I picked two spots and made sure I could always see them so I wouldn't get lost. I'm not stupid, Kane."

"I never said—"

But he'd thought it, he realized, chagrined.

She stared up at him and he found himself…speechless. He'd always been a pushover for big baby blues. Serena James had about the prettiest eyes he'd ever seen. Still he couldn't have her wandering off in the wilderness in her condition. He looked away, checking her head. At least her scalp wound had stopped bleeding.

"You could have gotten disoriented, passed out—"

She arched her eyebrows. "Eaten by bears?"

He scowled. "It's not funny. Too many things can happen out here. We're not in the city anymore. Even if you reached 911, we're a long way from any type of emergency service."

"I just wanted to help."

"Putting yourself in more danger is not helping."

"More danger than, say, being stranded up in the mountains in the middle of a snowstorm?"

"It's not snowing."

She gave him a pointed look. "Yet."

Kane hated to admit it, but she was right. He needed to get them both to shelter before the temperatures dipped further.

"Come on, we'll go back to the plane. The fuselage is

damaged, but I can rig something that will keep any rain out and block the wind some."

"What about the log cabin at the end of the meadow?" she asked.

"What log cabin?"

She pointed. "You can see it from up there."

This could be exactly what they needed. Kane straightened. "Show me."

Tottering on her heels through the snow, she led him a few yards farther up the slope. Visible through the trees, at the other end of the meadow was a small rustic-looking log cabin. The kind hunters or hikers might use. Snow drifted across the doorway but the roof looked secure enough. There even seemed to be an outhouse out back. Finally luck was on their side.

The cabin had to be warmer than the damaged plane.

Especially if those dark clouds now overhead decided to drop rain or snow.

"Looks good," he said. "Let's go."

"You're welcome," she said.

"What?"

"I thought you were thanking me for finding shelter."

"Yeah, I'll be real grateful tonight if the roof doesn't cave in."

"Tonight?" A slight tremor sounded in her voice. Her brows drew together, her forehead wrinkling. "Aren't we going to be rescued soon?"

Not wanting to scare her, he shrugged. "Probably not."

"Aren't you supposed to stay with your vehicle if you're lost?"

"Not if your vehicle won't keep you warm and dry through the night. We can leave a signal," he offered. "An SOS in the snow and an arrow pointing to the cabin in case the searchers arrive at daybreak. The two are close enough together it shouldn't be a problem."

Though the chances of being found tomorrow morning in this kind of weather were slim to none.

The corners of her mouth turned up. Appeased for now. Good.

"So what do we do now?" Serena asked.

"We make a signal, gather supplies and get to the cabin before dark."

Climbing down the hill, Serena struggled in her high-heeled boots, but she didn't complain, didn't sigh, didn't grimace. She trudged downward without saying a word. His respect inched up. She was tough.

More like stubborn, he told himself. What if she slipped? She could hurt her ribs more or something else.

As she picked her way over a fallen sapling, he grabbed her elbow to steady her. "Watch your step."

She snatched her arm away. "I can manage on my own."

"Yeah, until you fall on that cute little ass of yours."

She glared and marched away, her hips swaying under her brown and pink plaid wool coat.

Stubborn, Kane thought again. But the ass was definitely cute.

Serena had already made enough mistakes in the past seven months to last a lifetime. Stuck here in the middle of who-knew-where, she wasn't going to make another. Her boots sank into the snow as she made her way down the mountain. That meant keeping her distance from Kane Wiley.

Being in his arms, feeling the heat and strength emanating from him had been enough to send her senses spinning earlier. Serena turned up the collar of her coat.

Oh, she wanted to blame the reaction on her head injury, on the circumstances surrounding the emergency landing, on the relief of being alive. But she'd felt this way about him before they'd almost died, when she'd been sitting in the cockpit.

The man was as dangerous on the ground as he had been in the air. At least until he started up with all the manly, macho, I'm-in-charge attitude.

…until you fall on that cute little ass of yours.

Some nerve, but he was right about the falling part. One wrong step and she could do more than land flat on her face or bottom. All her plans, so meticulously put together over the years, could literally fall apart. Circumstances could change in an instant. One wrong decision could affect her entire future. Especially when the wrong man entered one's life. She'd seen that happen. She wouldn't allow that to happen to her.

"I'm…" Fine was on the tip of her tongue once again, but a glimpse at the wilderness surrounding her—natural, raw, untamed—made her feel anything but fine. She had never been more scared in her life, but she'd die before letting Kane know that. She looked at him. "I'm…okay."

Or would be, sooner or later.

She hoped.

Right now, she felt like a quivering mass of goo inside. Sheer willpower was getting her down this mountainside. Nothing more. And that was, as she'd just told him, okay.

She prided herself on her self-reliance. Others counted on her, not the other way around. Serena would never forget what had happened to her sister when she'd given up everything, putting all her faith and trust into one man, the absolutely wrong man for her. Morgan had lost everything, including their parents' love and respect. Years later, her sister was still trying to recover and reinvent herself as she struggled to raise a child on her own. Their parents still hadn't fully forgiven her lapse in…judgment.

No way did Serena want Kane's assistance. The only thing she needed was a new plan to get her through this ordeal.

One night in a cabin with him.

No. Big. Deal.

The more times she told herself that, the better.

"Are you warm enough?" he asked.

That depended on the definition of enough. Her feet tingled, the familiar pins and needles sensation after sitting in one place too long, and her fingers ached. She shoved her hands deeper into her jacket pockets. That helped. A little.

"Yes," she replied. "Are you?"

"I'm nice and toasty." Kane's mouth curved slightly, and his smile sent a warm rush through her. Too much charm, too little substance. "This little hike warmed me right up."

She focused on his eyes, serious and intent. "Glad it helped you."

"I'm going to make an SOS and an arrow pointed at the cabin out of rocks and branches. As long as it doesn't snow, someone might see it from the air."

"I'll help," she offered.

"Your ribs. Head."

"If it hurts, I'll stop."

Carefully Serena kneeled, picked up a rock sticking out of the snow and stood. A knife-edged pain sliced through her midsection. The freezing rock burned her already cold hands. She nearly dropped the rock.

"You okay?" Kane asked.

Not trusting her voice at the moment, she nodded. Serena mustered every ounce of strength to carry the rock to where Kane stood without dropping it or crying out.

"Gather tree branches for the arrow." He removed the gloves from his hands. "Put these on."

"I can't take your gloves."

He dropped the pair at her feet and walked away.

Serena stared at the black gloves lying on the snow. She didn't get him. Not at all. She put them on.

As they worked, the temperature dropped. Finally both symbols were finished. Not a moment too soon. Serena could barely catch her breath. She needed to sit.

"Let's get the supplies from the plane. I'll pull out your suitcase."

"Thanks." Serena wished she were strong enough to get her own bag. Not that any of those clothes packed away were appropriate attire for this weather or situation. Nor were any of them clean. Well, except for a pair of panties. She'd packed an extra. Thank goodness. And then she remembered. "We need to bring the dresses."

"No."

"Yes." She pointed out the tear in the fuselage, not that he was looking at her. "If moisture gets inside the cabin, the dresses could be ruined."

"We can cover them up."

"With what?" She mentally counted the days until Callie's wedding. Serena shuddered. "The dresses must come with us."

"We don't need wedding dresses to survive."

"The company does."

"Belle's company."

"Yes."

A beat passed.

"Fine," Kane said. "You want them, you carry them. You'll have to leave your clothes. I'm going to have my hands full with supplies."

"Fine." Serena felt anything but. Why did he have to be such a jerk about this?

Inside the cabin of the plane, she unhooked the dress bags. She moved slowly to keep from aggravating her sore ribs.

A noise caught Serena's attention. She looked over. Kane filled a duffel bag with the supplies.

"We need to hurry." He stuffed blankets into the bag. "The sky looks like it's going to open up any minute."

She counted the bags like a mother hen checking her chicks. Six. "I've got all of them."

"Come on then."

Serena struggled to climb out of the plane with the dress bags in her hands.

Kane snorted in disgust and took them from her. "Go."

When she was on the ground, he handed over the bulky gowns, tossed down the duffel, and jumped after it.

Serena clutched the bags, unsure what to do with them. She struggled to keep them out of the snow. Kane lifted another box through the plane's hatch before closing it behind him. He swung the strap of the duffel bag over his shoulder. "Move it."

He strode in the direction of the cabin, leaving deep tracks in the snow.

Serena stood frozen in place. Between the dresses, her injuries and the distance she needed to walk, she felt overwhelmed. It wasn't that far, but still…

He glanced back. "What are you waiting for?"

Mr. Right.

Someone to take the bags out of her hands, to tell her

everything would be okay and to love her from this day forward no matter what she said or did.

The lump in her throat matched the knot in her heart. Her vision blurred.

Oh, no, Serena didn't want to start crying. That was not part of their deal. And definitely not part of her image. She stared up at the sky, the dark clouds thicker than before, and blinked.

"Serena?" Kane called.

"I'm coming." What else was she going to do? Stay here? That would probably please Kane to no end. Blowing out a disgusted breath, she adjusted the bulky bags in her arms. No matter, she could handle this. She would save the dresses herself. Serena walked toward him. "Right behind you."

And that was where she stayed. Behind him.

Keeping up with Kane wasn't easy. Clumsy and hurting, she struggled to hold the bulky dresses and walk at the same time. She stumbled in the deep snow. Bit back a sigh. Swallowed a cry for help.

And hated every minute of it.

She repositioned the dress bags in her arms. The dark sky overhead looked ominous and threatening.

Kane walked back to her. He swore, muttering under his breath. "I knew this was going to happen."

"I've got them." Well, sort of.

He placed the box on the snow and took the dresses from her. "Carry the supplies."

He trudged toward the cabin without a glance back, the dress bags billowing over his arms, the heavy duffel banging his hip. Relieved, she wiped the corner of her eye and picked up the box.

She still had trouble walking straight, but the box was lighter and easier to handle than the dress bags.

No matter what she might think of him, attractive or not, a gentleman or a ladies' man, a nice guy or a jerk, he had saved the dresses by carrying them. Serena would toast Kane at the upcoming poker and margarita night the Belles held each month. The next one, she remembered with a pang, would also be a surprise bridal shower for Callie at Regina's house.

Callie.

Serena had to keep her gown safe.

Halfway to the cabin, a mix of sleet and snow poured from the sky, stinging her cheeks and chilling her lungs. The scent of ice permeated the air. Forget that it was only November. Winter had arrived. Those dress bags had better be waterproof as advertised.

With each step, the conditions deteriorated. Damp hair clung to her face. Her jacket felt heavier. The box in her hands weighed her down. She had no sense of direction.

"We're almost there," Kane yelled. "Do you see the cabin?"

She scanned the horizon, but all she could see was white in every direction. A burst of panic rioted through her. "No."

"Eleven o'clock."

Serena squinted in that direction. More white. And then the roofline came into focus. Thank goodness. "I see it."

"Don't lose sight of the cabin."

She didn't want to lose sight of him. A bone-deep chill overtook her, made it harder to breathe and walk, but she forged ahead, carried by fear and responsibility. Her numb fingers, in their borrowed gloves, cried out in pain. Guiltily she wondered how Kane's hands were faring, especially carrying the gowns.

The gowns. If Serena couldn't get to the cabin and Kane came back after her with the dresses they would get wetter. She quickened the pace.

And fell flat on her butt.

Just as Kane had predicted she would.

She sat on the snow empty-handed and struggling to breath. "Please don't turn around."

He didn't.

Kane reached the cabin and pushed his shoulder against the door. A banging sound echoed.

If he opened the door, he would look back.

Every muscle ached. Her ribs hurt. She couldn't catch her breath. But her pride was stronger than her physical ailments.

Using every ounce of strength she could muster, Serena stood. Pain radiated through her stomach. She waited for the hurt to subside, then brushed the snow off her bottom.

Thank goodness Kane was still trying to get into the cabin. Each of his attempts boomed through the meadow.

She gathered the supplies that had fallen onto the snow, put them back into the box and marched to the cabin.

By the time she arrived, the door was open. Kane stood outside, brushing the snow and ice off the dress bags.

"The dresses," she said.

"Get inside."

His harsh tone made her wince. The sound matched his dark eyes.

Serena did as she'd been told without a word.

She placed the box of supplies on a wooden table with chairs pushed under it. Her breath hung on the cold, stale air. The temperature inside the one-room cabin was warmer than outside, but not by much. She left her wet coat on.

Kane stepped inside. He hung the dress bags on one of the two sets of metal bunk beds along the wall opposite the door. Four beds but only one mattress.

She gulped. What had she gotten herself into?

"There must be a propane tank somewhere for the two wall lamps, the stovetop and oven." He removed the duffel bag from around his shoulder and picked up some sort of tube that was on the table. "I need to insert the chimney so we can use the woodstove and remove the shutters to get some air and light in here. I'll be right back."

Serena stood in near darkness. She noticed a wood cupboard. She opened it up and found cans of food. Not quite all the comforts of home, but they would be warm here and wouldn't starve. If you didn't mind rustic, the cabin was almost quaint and cozy with its log walls, beamed ceilings and small wood-paned windows. With the right companion, one might even find the place romantic.

She heard noises on the roof and on the two sides of the cabin where the windows were.

Several long minutes later, Kane came back in, carrying a stack of wood. He pulled off his jacket and hung it on a hook behind the door.

"No leaking holes in this roof, unlike my plane." As Kane opened the door to the stove, the hinges creaked. "You done good, Blondie."

Serena swallowed. "You, too."

"We're in this together."

She nodded.

He grabbed a newspaper from the duffel bag, crumpled a few pages up and stuck them inside the stove. Next he added a few smaller logs from the stash of dry wood sitting next to the stove and put them in. He pulled out a lighter from a pocket in his bag. The paper caught fire. A burst of heat warmed her from five feet away. The crackling sound and smell of burning wood filled the air.

Serena would never take domestic central heating for granted again. She removed the wet gloves.

"Stand closer to the stove," he said.

She did, placing her icy hands over the top. As the heat warmed her fingers, she wiggled all ten digits. "Thanks."

Next he lit the two wall lamps, filling the cabin with light. Kane didn't stop there. He poured a bottle of water into a pan and placed the pot on the stovetop. "You'll feel better once you drink something hot."

"What about you?" she asked, knowing he had to be as cold as she was.

He kicked off his shoes and removed his socks. "Let's get you warmed up first."

His concern for her well-being surprised Serena. He didn't seem the nurturing type. Still she hated being forced to depend on him for, well, everything.

A gust of wind rattled the windows. She shivered. If only the storm would go away so they could be found…

"You've done a great job getting us set up here." And she meant that. Serena was relieved he was with her.

Not many men—definitely not Rupert, who watched home improvement shows with her, but didn't own a toolbox, or Malcolm, who got weekly manicures—would know what to do in a situation like this. Rupert would be going crazy without being able to use his BlackBerry or laptop. Malcolm would be so inspired by the surroundings to design a line of casual outdoor wear that he wouldn't worry about anything else, including survival.

At least Kane, the poster boy for Mr. Oh-So-Wrong,

knew how to get them through a white-out, break into the cabin and get a fire going so they would have a warm, dry place to stay tonight and food. Yes, she could be in worse hands. An unfamiliar, yet content feeling settled over her.

"Warmed up enough?" Kane asked.

"For what?"

"To get undressed."

CHAPTER FIVE

SERENA wrapped her arms over her chest. "Get undressed?"

He scowled, feeling like an idiot. "You're not that irresistible, babe. We need to get out of our wet clothes to avoid hypothermia. That's all."

With the caked, dried blood on her forehead and face, she looked as if she'd fought a long, hard battle. Still, she raised her chin. "I don't have any other clothes to wear."

Serena had been polite up until now. Stubborn, yes, but composed. He appreciated that. She'd even tried to lift rocks with her ribs hurting. Kane respected that. But the way she stared down her nose at him like some ice princess irritated the hell out of him. The last thing he wanted, the last thing he needed, was to be responsible for someone else, especially a wide-eyed blonde who reminded him of his worst mistakes.

"You've got six wedding dresses to choose from," he said. "Take your pick."

Her mouth gaped.

"You chose the gowns over your clothes. Someone should get some use out of them."

"Someone will. The very lucky women I designed them

for." Her eyes never left his. "Which is why I'm not parading around a dirty, cold cabin in a couture wedding gown."

"Fine." Kane had just been rattling her chain, anyway. He opened the jam-packed duffel bag, pulled out a blanket and a shirt and tossed them to her. "Here."

"You want me to wear these?"

"It's all we've got. I left most of my clothes in the plane so I could bring supplies." Kane failed to mention he'd only brought clothes for himself. He wasn't used to thinking about someone else. "You can have the pants. I'll wear the blanket."

"That's okay. I don't need to change." She flapped the sides of her skirt like a flamenco dancer. "I'm drying off."

"Yeah, right." Her coat looked like a sopping wet, oversize dishrag. Droplets fell from the hem of her skirt. Her sad excuse for boots were completely water soaked. Not good for warming her up. "Take your clothes off now or I'll take them off for you."

Her mouth gaped. "What did you say?"

"You heard me." He opened the first aid kit he'd packed in the duffel bag. "Hypothermia is nothing to mess around with. Your speech slurs, your breathing slows down, your skin becomes pale and cold, you shiver uncontrollably and you feel lethargic and confused. In its final stages, you feel so hot you rip your clothes off to cool down. But by then it's usually too late."

"Too late?"

"To recover."

A beat passed. She tried to remove her coat, wincing with every movement.

After her third attempt, Kane cursed. He did not need

this. Her. He grabbed hold of the collar. "You're going to hurt yourself more."

Carefully he drew the coat down her arms and over her hands. She didn't grimace, but he could tell she was hurting.

He put the jacket on another of the hooks on the back of the cabin door. "This thing weighs a ton. I can't believe you hiked all the way here wearing it."

"I didn't have a choice."

"True, but you're stronger than you look."

"Thank you," she mumbled.

"Sit." He moved an empty chair closer to the stove. "I'll take your boots off then you can undress."

Serena sat, still and silent, as if waiting for a jury to declare her innocence or guilt. She clutched the blanket and shirt in her lap.

"Left or right?" Kane asked.

She raised her right foot. He pulled on the tall boot. The wet leather clung to her thin calf and didn't budge. She gripped the seat of the chair.

"This might hurt," he said.

"Just get them off." A hint of vulnerability flickered in her eyes. "Please."

Her plea hit him hard in the gut.

"You got it." Kane peeled the leather off, folding it over toward her ankle. He tugged until the boot came off. "Next."

She raised her left foot. Removing that one was easier now that he knew what to do.

"Now your—" he stared at her feet "—nylons?"

As she reached under her skirt, his groin tightened. What the hell was she doing? And how could he get a better look? He tilted his head.

Serena rolled something down her leg. "Thigh highs."

Despite the chill lingering in the air and his wet clothes, his temperature shot up twenty degrees. Time to get back to business. "I need to check your ribs."

"My ribs are better."

"Your breathing's off."

"Do you make a habit of staring at women's chests?"

"Every chance I get," he admitted cheerfully. "Come on, let's have a look."

Her mouth tightened. "You're a pilot, not a doctor."

"Right," he admitted. "But I've played doctor before."

Serena stared at him.

Okay, he'd cut her some slack for having no sense of humor right now. "You like being in control and taking care of yourself, right?"

She nodded.

"I'm the same way. I'm used to being on my own, not having to worry about anyone else, but sometimes life throws you a curveball and you have to make the best of it. I'm all you've got, Blondie," he said. "So lift your shirt."

"Does that line ever work?" she asked.

"You'd be amazed."

"I'd be astonished." A corner of her mouth lifted. "You really need to work on your bedside manner."

Finally a crack in the princess's ice.

He bit back a smile. "You think?"

"Most definitely." Serena raised her blouse enough to show an expanse of smooth skin and a flat belly.

Oh, man. Talk about sweet. The air rushed out of his lungs. His mouth went dry. He focused on her belly button—an innie.

"Kane?"

What was he doing? Staring? Leering?

Talk about a curveball. She was his passenger. His responsibility. He was stuck taking care of her whether he liked it or not. "Where does it hurt?"

Serena pointed to her left side. "Here."

He studied the spot, ignoring her creamy complexion and the curve of her waist. He pressed lightly, her skin soft against his fingers. "Does this hurt?"

"A little."

He moved to a different spot. "How about here?"

She winced. "Ouch."

Kane pulled his hand back. "I—"

"It's okay," she said before he could apologize. "Really."

"You could have fractured a rib, but it's likely they're just bruised. There's no way to tell without an X-ray." He opened the first aid kit. Fully stocked. At least he was prepared. "I'm going to wrap you with an Ace bandage to be on the safe side. Stand up."

She did and raised her blouse higher. He glimpsed the lace edge of her bra—pink, but who was noticing?—and sucked in a breath.

Don't look. Don't think. Just get it done.

Wrapping the bandage around her ribs, he mentally recited the multiplication table for nine, ten and eleven. "How does that feel? Too tight?"

She looked as uncomfortable as he felt. "Just right."

Was it? Kane hoped so. He didn't want to hurt her.

He secured the end. "All done."

"Thanks," she mumbled.

Outside the storm raged, the wind blew and icy pellets hit the cabin. The forced intimacy of the situation only added to the tension inside. The lack of conversation didn't help. The burning logs crackled. The water boiled. The sounds and sight of their breathing filled the air.

It had been a long day. It would be an even longer night.

"Let's clean your cut." He washed away the dried blood with an antiseptic wipe, dabbed antibiotic cream on the cut and placed two butterfly bandages over the long gash. She didn't flinch or complain. "All done. It's not too bad, but you might have a little scar."

"A scar?" She sounded concerned.

"Maybe, right near your temple. It's hard to tell."

She reached up, but he grabbed hold of her hand. "Don't touch."

"But—"

"A little Vitamin E oil can go a long way." He released her hand. "Though guys dig chicks with scars."

"Not all men. Some guys find an imperfection and leave."

"Idiots," Kane muttered. "You'd be better off without a man like that. Scars show a person takes risks and isn't afraid to live. Very cool in my book."

She gazed up at him. "You mean that?"

"Yep."

A shy smile graced her lips. "Thanks."

"No problem." He grabbed the dry pants, a pair of khakis. "You want them?"

"No, thanks," she said. "I'll stick with what I have."

"You can dress by the stove. I'll be over there."

By the bunk beds, he unbuckled his belt and unzipped his pants. As he pulled them off, he heard another zipper— Serena's skirt?—and the rustling of fabric.

"If something's wet, even damp, take it off." He removed his underwear and torn shirt. "We can hang our clothes on the hooks and purlins so they'll be dry in the morning."

"Okay."

Kane almost laughed. Nothing about this was okay, especially standing naked in a cold cabin, miles away from civilization, with a beautiful woman he wanted nothing to do with. He pulled on the dry pants and zipped them. "You dressed?"

The sound of fabric ripping filled the air. "Almost."

The scent of smoke lingered in the air, even though he'd opened the damper to the flue. Staring at the aged, dark wood walls of the cabin, Kane wondered who else had been forced to take refuge here during a winter storm. The items inside—food and firewood—suggested someone used the cabin. Maybe forest service employees checked the place routinely.

"I'm dressed," Serena said.

Kane turned. His mouth dropped open. Unbelievable. She looked like a Grecian princess with the blanket wrapped around her body and tied at the waist and at the top with sashes made from strips of the fabric. Absolutely beautiful.

"Wow." Forget about being cold. His temperature shot into the red zone. He remembered what she'd said about her dresses. "You can even make 'couture' out of a blanket."

"What can I say?" She put on his blue shirt, buttoned the front and rolled up the sleeves. The color brought out the blue of her eyes. "It's a gift."

Seeing her wearing his shirt was kind of sexy, too. "I'd say so."

He smiled at her.

She smiled back.

Time stopped. They could have been anywhere—the cabin, inside the plane, Seattle, Boston. The place didn't matter.

Only here, only now, only them.

The beat of his heart seemed stronger, the blood flowing through his veins warmer. He didn't want to have to take care of her. He didn't want to have to worry about her. But at this moment he wouldn't have wanted to be with anyone else.

The moment lingered.

Kane could have broken the contact, but didn't want to. He hadn't felt this connected to someone in…well, ever.

Finally Serena looked away, her gaze resting on the bunks for a few seconds before focusing on the wood-stove. "I guess now there's not much else to do except hit the sack. I mean, bed. You know, sleep. Somewhere."

She looked cute all flustered with her cheeks pink. Forget the ice princess glare or the Grecian princess attire, she was suddenly natural and approachable.

Too bad she was practically engaged or something.

"You can always make a nest out of those wedding dresses," he said to lighten the mood, to set some distance between them. "Lots of nice, comfy material there."

But instead of getting all prissy on him again, Serena laughed. "Obviously, you don't know much about wedding gown fabrics. Tulle is too scratchy and satin is too slippery. Silk wouldn't be too bad except for all the beading and appliqué. That might be uncomfortable."

His smile widened. "Then we'll have to share the bed."

That was what Serena was afraid he'd say. "I…"

"You have a boyfriend," Kane finished for her. "I understand."

But she didn't. And he couldn't.

"Using our body heat is the best way to keep each other warm," he explained.

The coal-size lump in her throat kept her from answering.

"You can trust me, Serena."

But did she trust herself? That was the real question. One she'd never worried about before. Serena had never understood what unknown trait made a totally wrong man so irresistible to a woman. She'd vowed never to allow herself to be in that position, never to make the same mistake her sister had.

Which meant figuring out how to handle this…dilemma. Serena fussed with the folds of the blanket she wore.

"Hungry?" he asked.

She nodded, rolling up the long-sleeved shirt more. Wearing Kane's shirt felt strange, and she wasn't sure she liked it.

He unwrapped the cellophane from a sandwich. "Turkey and Swiss cheese, okay?"

"My favorite actually." She stared at the sandwich he placed in front of her. "Thanks."

He sat at the table with a sandwich of his own. "We have two more sandwiches, a bunch of fruit and enough pre-packaged snacks to last a week."

"Plus all the canned goods in the cupboard. We aren't going to starve."

They ate quickly without saying a word to one another. She didn't mind the silence. Not when she needed to figure out a solution to the sleeping arrangement problem, one that didn't involve a long, cold night shivering on the table or floor. She had to think of something.

The alternative…

Serena didn't want to feel Kane's bare, broad shoulders and chest against her. She didn't want to feel his heart beat. She didn't want to breathe his warm breath. Those things were too intimate, too dangerous.

"What if we slept head to toe, in the opposite directions?" she suggested. "We'd still be able to share body heat, but not…"

Time to stop babbling. The less she said the better. A mouse scurried across the floor. She didn't scream, but she lifted her feet.

"Not a bad suggestion," he said, not seeming to notice the mouse. "But you don't want your nose anywhere near my feet. Besides, our good parts will still be in contact."

"True." She rubbed her hands together. "I'm just—"

"Nervous?"

"A little." More like a lot. "Silly, I know."

He pulled out another blanket. "Once you feel how warm it is when we're both in the bed, all your doubts will disappear."

That's what she was afraid of.

Still Serena knew he was right. Keeping warm was the most important thing.

She crawled onto the lower bunk. The mattress, more like a pad, sank from her weight.

"Give me a shove if I snore," he said.

"Uh, sure." She didn't want to touch him, let alone shove him. "But I'm so tired I probably won't notice anything."

Facing the log wall, she squeezed her eyes shut. She wanted sleep to come quickly and easily tonight.

Something creaked. The floor? The roof? Something bigger than a mouse? She opened her eyes. Black, total darkness as if the moon and stars had been sucked into a vacuum. She couldn't see her hand. He must have turned off the lamps.

Serena lay there. She smelled smoke and heard the burning logs in the stove. She also felt a presence nearby.

Kane.

The mattress sank to the right. He crawled in.

His foot brushed hers and tingles shot up her leg. "Oops," he said.

The tingles didn't stop. "It's a little cramped."

"Better than the floor."

"Or a chair." She didn't want to sound as if she were complaining. He shouldn't have to put up with that after today, even if the only thing she wanted to do was get on a wide-body plane with four engines, at least two pilots and three hundred passengers and fly home.

Far away from this wilderness nightmare.

Far, far away from Kane.

"It could be worse," he said.

She rolled toward him. "What?"

"It could be worse," Kane repeated.

The wind howled, blowing snow against the cabin, the noises outside as unfamiliar as the complete darkness inside. Thinking about the emergency landing sent a chill shivering down her spine. This could not be any worse unless one of them had been seriously injured or worse. "Thank you for landing the plane, Kane, and coming after me and…"

"Just doing my job."

He sounded so nonchalant after saving their lives. "It was more than that."

"You've done well yourself," he said. "Finding this cabin."

"Sure beats the airplane."

"I'll say." He rolled onto his side. The motion sent her falling back against him. She scooted away. Well, as away as she could manage on a twin-size bed. "But you would have managed in the plane tonight if it'd come to that."

"No, I wouldn't," she whispered.

Serena cringed. She couldn't believe she'd said the words out loud.

His body drew closer. "Why do you say that?"

She was afraid to move. Breathe. "It's just—"

"What?"

This was so hard, but after all he'd done for her today she owed him this much. "I'm not exactly the type to just go with it, without quite a bit of…planning and preparation."

"You've been doing okay here with very little prep time."

His compliment pleased her. More than it should. "Thanks."

"You're welcome," he said. "I'm more a seat-of-my-pants type of guy."

I like to go where I want to go.

She remembered what he'd said in the cockpit, about his need for freedom. "We're very different."

"Yes, we are."

His words made her feel sad for some reason. Isolated by the snow and wilderness, cut off from everything and everyone familiar, she wanted to be like Kane. If she could be more like him, this "situation" might not be so hard to handle.

"We'll get through this," he reassured. "Go to sleep."

Not such an easy thing to do when lying next to him felt so good. Better than it should.

His body heat warmed the space next to her. She heard the rasp of his breathing, the beat of his heart. Letting her guard down and drifting off to sleep probably wasn't the smartest course of action.

Not when she felt safe and secure with Kane. Two ways she never thought she'd ever feel with a man like him. They might be different, but those differences made her feel better and more at ease.

Out here where she didn't belong, Serena knew he would take care of her. Make sure they survived. She survived. Whether she wanted his help or not.

And for that she was grateful.

More than he would ever know.

On Monday morning, Belle stepped into the reception area of the shop with anticipation. She couldn't wait to find out more about the bridal show, though she knew Serena was coming in late.

Julie, her auburn hair a mass of corkscrew curls, sat at the front desk preparing for the day. Natalie set out cake samples for the Belles to taste when they arrived.

"Good morning," Belle said. "What are we sampling today?"

"Banana cake with custard parfait filling." Two rainbow-striped pencils held Natalie's blond hair on top of her head. "The girls wanted me to do something with bananas so I figured why not. Of course, they wanted a chocolate filling."

Belle grinned, imagining the eight-year-old twins asking their mom to bake them a special cake. She wondered if they helped or just made a mess with the flour like the last time.

"Things are looking up businesswise this morning,"

Julie said. "We have four appointments scheduled today and a full inbox of e-mail requests for information."

Belle clapped her hands together. "Fantastic news."

"What's going on?" Audra asked as she walked into the shop, carrying a leather briefcase on her shoulder and holding a coffee in her hand. Sleek with long blond hair, she looked more like one of their clients than a certified public accountant.

"Just the usual Monday catch-up." Natalie handed Audra a plate. "Taste this."

"It's not yet nine and already I'm loading up on calories. Not that I mind. No one's looking at these hips." Audra took a bite. Sighed. "This is absolutely incredible. Your best yet."

"I'll remember that when you get married."

Audra set her fork on the plate. "I'm never getting married."

"That makes two of us then," Natalie said. "I've got my hands full with the twins. I couldn't imagine having to add a boyfriend let alone a husband into the mix."

Julie frowned. "Don't say that."

"I agree." Belle wanted each of her girls to have a happy ending. "You never know when love will come calling."

The doorbell rang. The four women looked at each other.

"How did you do that, Belle?" Audra asked.

Belle shrugged. "Probably just an appointment."

"Hmm." Julie checked the appointment book lying on the table. "We don't have any this early."

"I'll answer as long as it's not love calling for me." Audra opened the door. "Charlie?"

Charlie Wiley stood on the front step, looking anxious. "Is Belle here?"

The faint tremor in his voice worried Belle. She had never seen him look so upset, not even when she wouldn't sell him her late husband, Matthew's, vintage Rolls-Royce. "I'm right here. What's wrong?"

His brown eyes glistened with tears. He opened his mouth to speak, but no words came out.

Belle touched his arm. "Are you okay?"

He nodded, swallowed. "Kane and Serena never made it back from Seattle last night."

Julie gasped. "Where are they?"

"Has anyone heard from them?" Audra asked.

Natalie covered her mouth with her hands. "Oh, no."

Panic rioted through Belle. Fear clogged her throat. She loved all the Belles like daughters. "Do you have any idea where they might be?"

"The control center received a distress call. Kane was going to make an emergency landing, but that was the final transmission," Charlie said. "The plane's last known position places them somewhere over Idaho."

Audra's forehead creased. "Last known position?"

Charlie grimaced. "Kane and Serena's plane is officially missing."

CHAPTER SIX

HALF asleep, Kane snuggled against the inviting warmth and feminine softness of the body next to him. He could get used to waking up like this, his legs tangled in hers.

She had her back to him, her feet tucked between his legs.

His hand rested on the curve of her hip, the fabric of her makeshift skirt separating skin from skin. He opened his eyes, but didn't move. Not even his hand.

Serena.

Waking up with her so close in this small bed was…nice.

Yeah, nice.

As if he were sleeping with a cuddly puppy or something. A puppy would be better than an attractive, sexy woman with a serious boyfriend. What the hell was he thinking? Doing?

He untangled himself and crawled off the lower bunk. Faint light shone through the wood-paned windows. Morning already? Kane felt as if he'd only closed his eyes a few minutes ago.

Outside, a blanket of fresh white powder covered the ground, trees and bushes. It looked like a Christmas card.

Pain ricocheted through Kane as he remembered Christmases with his mother. She would have been frantic right now if she'd been alive and he was missing. He thought about his dad. Had his father been notified of the situation? Were people searching for them yet?

The overcast skies didn't fill Kane with much hope for rescue this morning, but at least it wasn't snowing anymore. Their signals could have been covered, though. He might as well take advantage of the break in the weather and head back to the plane.

Kane glanced back at Serena. She slept soundly, a hint of a smile on her face. He wondered what she dreamed about. Shopping and weddings? Or something more, deeper, secret?

A warm feeling settled over him. He shook it off.

He dressed in his clothes from yesterday, now dry, added a log to the woodstove so she wouldn't wake up cold and put on his shoes.

"Where are you going?" Serena asked softly.

"To the plane," he said. "It's stopped snowing. I'm going to check on our signal, bring back more supplies. Clothes."

She sat up on her elbows, looking sleep-rumpled and adorable. "Want me to go with you?"

"Stay here. You can help me later, okay?"

Serena nodded.

"How are your ribs?" he asked.

"Not as sore."

"Good. Probably bruised then, not broken," he said. "Go back to sleep."

She closed her eyes and rolled over away from him.

Kane watched her for a moment, noticing her long, graceful neck, then forced himself out into the cold. He hiked back to the plane, unable to see his and Serena's footprints from yesterday due to the weather overnight.

Not a good sign.

At the plane, he couldn't see the SOS or the arrow. He spent five minutes trying to locate the rocks and branches and another ten brushing and kicking off the snow. His effort felt like a lesson in futility given the thick, dark cloud-covered sky above. It was going to start snowing any minute. But if Serena asked about the signals, he wanted to tell her the truth.

Who knew? Maybe a plane was looking for them right now. The thought made him light a fire in the middle of the snow-covered meadow far away from any trees or plants. Smoke might be easier for others to see than the SOS, arrow or plane.

As smoke drifted up to the sky, Kane turned his attention to the plane. He stared at the crippled aircraft covered in white. "Damn."

He'd known the damage had been bad, but seeing the plane this morning… He wanted to punch something. Disappointment crashed into him. Frustration burned. He'd lost everything.

No, not everything.

He was still here. Serena, too. No reason to lose control.

Kane entered the plane and looked for anything that might come in handy, including the clothes he'd removed from his duffel bag yesterday. He found his camera in the pile and took pictures of the plane in case the insurance company needed them. By the time he had finished and closed the door to the plane, snowflakes were falling from the sky and the fire was dying.

So much for a break in the weather.

Kane unloaded Serena's suitcase and his second bag.

He noticed items from the bridal show. He remembered candles from the booth and took out the two boxes. There might be other stuff they could use. Something that might make Serena more comfortable. Besides, he should take all he could. This might be his last trip back to the plane today.

The snow fell faster, harder.

Or tomorrow.

"The weather has grounded the air operation, but they plan to get a land search under way once they determine the search grid," Charlie said later that morning after a telephone conversation with the county sheriff in charge of the search and rescue operation. "I'm flying west."

Belle's insides clenched. She walked to the window of her apartment above The Wedding Belles' shop. On the street below, life went on. A car honked. People hurried along the sidewalks. A taxi pulled up to the curb. Two well-dressed women exited. But inside her building, everything—except hope and prayers—had stopped.

"Of course you're going," she said.

Belle wouldn't expect any less from Charlie. She understood he needed to go, to be closer to where his son was, but a part of her hated to see him leave. His presence at the shop this morning had been a blessing to her and her girls.

"Did you speak with Serena's parents?" he asked.

"Yes. They are somewhere in the Himalayas. They decided that by the time they make it to an airport let alone fly back, this will probably all be over with so they are continuing on their trek." Belle's heart ached for her young designer. Pleasing her parents and gaining their approval was important to Serena. She included them in all her triumphs. And now they were too busy to come when their daughter needed them most? Belle didn't understand that. "They asked me to pass on information as I hear it. Will you keep me updated?"

He walked to her and linked his fingers with hers. His touch comforted. His hand felt warm and strong against her skin. "I want you to come with me."

Her heart bumped. "Me?"

"Yes, you." Charlie squeezed her hand. When he let go, she missed the unexpected contact. "Serena might want a familiar face around when she's found."

"Oh, she definitely needs someone there for her."

"So you'll go?" he asked.

For Serena's sake, Belle wanted to say yes, but she'd heard the anticipation in Charlie's voice and she couldn't forget the way her heart had reacted when he'd invited her. She wanted to go with him for her own sake as much as Serena's. And that concerned Belle. "Let me talk to Serena's boyfriend first. If he can't go, I will."

Serena stared out of the cabin window. With all the white on the ground and falling from the sky, she couldn't see anything. She couldn't see Kane. "Where are you?"

She rubbed her arms to fight a shiver. She'd changed back into her own clothes. Wearing Kane's shirt felt too…intimate, but now she felt like putting it back on. Anything to feel closer to him. She didn't like being left alone out here. She didn't like any of this.

Not that she was throwing herself a pity party. That wasn't her style. She'd managed to do a couple of things this morning: visiting the outhouse, trying to find reception on her cell phone, brushing her teeth and setting out breakfast—fruit, granola bars and raisins.

But with Kane gone for so long and the weather turning bad again, all she could do now was wait and think. What if he didn't come back?

Needing to do something, she forced herself away from the window, organized the food and tidied the cabin the best she could. But thoughts of Kane never left her mind. "Come back, please."

The minutes dragged.

Finally she heard a noise outside. The storm or…

Serena opened the door. A gust of wind blew snow and cold air inside, pushing the door back into the cabin. She didn't care. Not when she saw Kane pulling her suitcase like a sled through the snow. Piled on top were boxes and a duffel bag.

Relief filled her, but she played it cool. Easy to do with the snow falling hard and fast. Goose bumps prickled her skin. She should have put on her coat, but seeing him sent warmth surging through her veins. "Back already?"

"You're going to get cold." His mouth tightened. "Where are your coat and shoes?"

Why had she wanted him to come back? Serena sighed. "I want to help. Hand me something."

He hesitated for a moment then handed her one of the boxes. "Watch your ribs."

"They're not hurting, but I'll be careful."

She helped him unload the supplies. Together they moved everything inside in less than three minutes.

Kane closed the door, shutting out the storm and sealing them inside. "Thanks for the help."

With his rugged good looks, razor stubble on his face and strong body, he looked like a renegade mountain man. Rough, raw, wild. All he needed was a rifle, boots and parka to complete the picture.

"You're welcome." Serena fought the urge to brush off the snow still in his hair. Personality aside, even a casual touch wouldn't be a good idea. He might not be the kind of man she wanted in her life, but she couldn't deny his appeal. "You brought back a lot of stuff."

"It'll save me a trip later."

"Smart thinking." And that would save her from worrying about being alone. "But it's almost like moving day with all these things crammed in here."

"Did you just move?"

"About a year ago," she said. "I have a flat in Back Bay."

He unpacked one of the boxes. "Must be nice."

"It is, but I'd rather have a house. One with a fireplace, a fenced yard, a sewing room and—" *a nursery* "—room for a family."

Serena ignored a twinge of disappointment that her plans weren't looking too good right now.

And hadn't been for a while.

"What about you?" She rummaged through her suitcase for any suitable or warmer clothing. "Where do you live?"

"As of now, here." Kane added a log to the fire. "What's with the food?"

Didn't he like it? Had she wasted their provisions? Or did he think she was trying too hard, like a woman who slipped from her lover's bed to make him pancakes?

Of course, Kane probably liked pancakes.

Serena would have settled for coffee.

She lifted her chin. "While you were gone, Bigfoot made breakfast."

"Looks good." Kane's grin reached his eyes. "Thanks, Sasquatch."

Okay, Serena felt better. And her tummy felt all tingly. Hungry. She must be hungry.

She recognized boxes from the bridal show. "Why did you bring these back?"

"To see if we could find anything useful inside." He bit into a granola bar.

She opened the first box and dug through the contents. Jackpot. "Oh. Wow."

"Candles?"

"Something better. Something you're going to like."

He popped a grape into his mouth. "What's that?"

She raised a small item wrapped in cellophane from the box. "Chocolate."

He wiped his hand over his forehead in an exaggerated gesture. "Now I can last at least another day."

Serena pulled out the pieces and placed them on the table. "We have more than enough for a few more days if worst comes to worst."

"Someone will come for us."

His words reassured her, gave her hope. "As soon as the weather breaks."

A slight hesitation, then a nod.

Uh-oh. "What's wrong?" she asked.

"Nothing's wrong," he said. "But finding us might take a few days even after the weather breaks."

Days, not a day. She chewed on the inside of her mouth.

"It's going to be okay, Serena."

"I'm sure things will be better now that we've found chocolate." She hoped she sounded lighthearted, even cheerful, in spite of the heaviness pressing down on the center of her chest.

"Much better."

Serena nodded. This was so out of her everyday routine, even her not-so-ordinary life. A picnic was about the closest she'd come to the outdoors in the last ten years. "And we have plenty of water to drink with all the snow."

"Just remember, don't eat the snow. Otherwise, your body wastes too many calories trying to melt it."

"How do you know all this?" she asked, impressed.

"I was a Boy Scout."

"Interesting." She tried to picture him fresh-faced with neatly trimmed hair and a sharply pressed uniform. Tried and failed. Though she could imagine him being a really cute little boy. "The Scouts seem like they would have been too structured for someone like you."

"Like me?"

"A...free spirit."

"I was just a kid. I didn't know the meaning of the word *free*. Scouting was what my dad and I did together back then."

"You must have had fun. Charlie's a great guy."

"He has his moments."

She thought about Kane's father and him wanting to buy Belle's late husband's old car. Even after she said no, Charlie kept coming around the shop. "We're all hoping Belle will go out with him."

Kane's brow furrowed. "I thought they were already dating."

"Not yet. Although not for your father's lack of trying."

"My father goes after what he wants. No matter what the consequences."

The bitterness lacing Kane's words surprised her. "Charlie doesn't seem so tunnel vision to me. He was okay when Belle wouldn't sell her car to him."

Kane shrugged.

"Either way," Serena said. "He must be so worried about you right now."

"Maybe. We aren't that close anymore. I don't see him much. Sometimes not at all."

She didn't understand. "But he's your father."

"He's done a few things I don't agree with."

Serena got a familiar sinking feeling in her stomach. "So what? You stay away from him because of that?"

Kane nodded. "He made his choices. He can live with the consequences."

Her heart dropped. Not another person, like her parents and others, who withheld love if disappointed. That was so unfair, so wrong. Serena had tried to make her parents see what they were doing, but they wouldn't listen. Maybe she could help Kane see what he was doing by holding a grudge. "I'm sure your father is frantic right now."

With a shrug, he finished his granola bar. "I'd bet Rupert is more worried about you."

Serena stared out the window. The news would only bring relief to her ex-boyfriend. No more bumping into her at the newest café or hippest club with a date by his side and having to deal with the ensuing awkwardness.

"Rupert…" Guilt coated her mouth at the thought of lying again. Her friends, her family, even Kane deserved better.

"What?" Kane asked.

The silence intensified the knot in her stomach. She listened to her breathing, to his, to the logs popping in the wood stove. "We're not… We… Rupert broke up with me in April."

There. She'd said it. And, surprisingly, her world hadn't exploded.

Instead a rare peace filled her heart. Finally someone knew the truth.

His eyes darkened. "Belle said—"

"No one knows," Serena interrupted.

"Why not?"

"Well…not telling anyone made sense at the time." She took a deep breath and exhaled slowly. "I planned to tell people, but I never could find the right opportunity. We decided to throw our assistant, Julie, a wedding. Everyone was so happy and trying to keep it a secret from her. I didn't want my news to spoil the fun. A little while later, our florist, Callie, fell in love and got engaged to this great guy named Jared. After that, our photographer, Regina, seemed to go through something with her husband, Dell, but now they are so happy and in love." Serena watched the snow falling from the sky. Each flake reminded her of the time that had passed. "And now, so many months have gone by, telling them seems like an even bigger deal than before."

"Your friends wouldn't care."

But Serena had cared. She hadn't wanted their sympathy. She didn't want their pity. She only wanted them to see her as a smart, successful woman who was on her way to having it all. "They will be disappointed."

He raised his eyebrows. "All because you aren't practically engaged?"

"Because I wasn't—" perfect "—the person they thought I was."

The person they liked. The person they depended on. The person she had taught and groomed herself to be—bright, capable, accomplished, without needs or flaws.

"What about The Suit?" Kane asked.

"The Suit?" And then she remembered. "Malcolm is a friend who would like us to become business partners."

"But he wouldn't mind more," Kane said. "And you?"

"I…" She thought about Malcolm. On paper she

couldn't ask for anything more, but she really didn't think of him as anything more than a friend. And though he was a great guy, she wasn't sure what kind of father he'd be. Dad-potential was an important quality for her Mr. Right. "Probably not."

"So no boyfriend?"

"No boyfriend." Serena stared at initials with a heart around them carved on the wood windowsill. She traced the engraving with her fingertip. Maybe V and J had found the true love she wanted so badly. "Pretty pathetic, huh?"

"That you don't have a boyfriend?"

Not having a boyfriend didn't bother her as much as how not having a boyfriend affected her plans. She shook her head. "That I lied."

"Not lied. More like withholding information." Kane rose from his chair. "And you had your reasons."

"It seemed so at the time."

He moved toward her, with purpose and intent. "You did it for your friends."

"I did."

"You weren't trying to hurt anyone." He stopped in front of her. "You wanted to help them by making sure they were happy."

"You nailed it." A smile tugged on the corners of her mouth. "And you also made me feel better. Thanks."

"Want me to keep making you feel better?" he asked.

She nearly laughed. Okay, maybe his personality wasn't so horrible. "Please do."

"I, for one, am really happy you're not dating Rupert or The Suit."

"Why?"

"Because if you were, I couldn't do this."

"Do…?"

His mouth covered hers before she could say another word. His lips pressed against hers with an urgency that took her breath away. Hunger, desire, need.

His kiss possessed.

She tasted salt, sweat, male. An intoxicating, addictive combination. One she couldn't get enough of.

His razor stubble scratched her face. She didn't care. Serena wrapped her arms around his neck and kissed him back. The kiss melded into another and another. She wanted to get closer to him.

As if reading her mind, Kane embraced her. He pressed lightly—perhaps remembering her injured ribs?—drawing her toward him. She went eagerly, wanting more.

She'd never known so much hunger; she'd never felt so complete. The emotions contradicted each other as a battle between mind and body warred inside her.

His arms tight around her, she wanted him even closer. But he was oh-so-wrong for her.

His tongue lingered, explored and caressed with such care, she could barely stand. But he wanted freedom at any cost.

His mouth against hers, she felt as if she could fly, soar and never have to come back to the ground. But he didn't love unconditionally.

Nothing made sense. Not him kissing her. Not her response to him kissing her.

But with his lips devouring hers, reason and common sense took a back seat. Nothing else mattered. Nothing except more kisses. She leaned into him, soaking up his strength and his warmth.

Gratitude. That had to be the explanation.

She was kissing Kane back as a way to repay him for all he'd done. But the blood boiling through her veins had nothing to do with thankfulness and everything to do with desire.

Kane kissed her as if she were what kept him alive—air, water, his heart. He made her feel so special. She didn't deserve it after lying about Rupert, but Kane didn't seem to mind.

He showered her with kiss after kiss after kiss as if this were her reward. She accepted. Gladly.

She'd kissed men before, of course, but all of those seemed like practice to prepare her for this…for the main event.

Everything about his kisses was perfect.

Everything except the man himself.

Serena didn't care.

Oh, she should care. No doubt she would care later.

But for now, for this very moment, she wouldn't think so much. She wouldn't analyze. She wouldn't plan.

She would simply…enjoy.

Enjoy the moment.

Enjoy the sensation.

Enjoy Kane.

The kisses continued, on and on. Thank goodness he had his arms around her or she might already be on the floor. He moved his lips from her mouth across her jaw to her ear. He nibbled on her earlobe. Tingles exploded like firecrackers. She gasped. Kane dragged his mouth away.

His breathing fast, his eyes dark, he stared at her. "I'm sorry. I shouldn't have done that. It won't happen again."

Those were the last words her tingling lips wanted to hear.

"But thank you," he added.

Serena hadn't known what to expect, but his saying thanks wasn't it. Granted, a man like Kane probably made out regularly with women. But he didn't even seem to like her much. Not enough to kiss her, but he acted as if she'd held open a door for him, not let him plunder and pillage her mouth. "You're welcome?"

He raised a hand to her face and brushed a strand of hair out of her eyes. "Ready?"

Her pounding heart accelerated. "For what?"

She sounded as breathless as she felt.

"To get to work."

If she had been a hot air balloon, she would have gone splat against the Earth. "Work?"

"We need to unpack, find wood for the stove, a lot of things."

No, she wanted to scream. Her lips felt swollen and bruised. Her insides still tingled. And he wanted to talk about getting to work? Not the kiss?

Serena straightened. If the kiss meant nothing to him, then it meant nothing to her. And maybe all wedding dresses next season would be hot-pink like Marsha Schumacher had wanted her gown to be. "Before we get to work, I have to ask. What was that all about?"

He looked at Serena expectantly.

"The, um, kiss," she added.

"An impulse," Kane said. "I just wanted to kiss you."

"You wanted to kiss me?"

"Yeah, you looked like you needed to be kissed. With no boyfriend in the picture there was nothing stopping me."

Okay. Not. "So is this something you do a lot? Kissing women who look like they need a kiss?"

"Not random women on the street. Well, except for this one time in Paris and another in Rome. But generally, with minor exceptions, the answer is no. I do not make a habit of kissing random women. And I only planned to kiss you once."

"What happened?" she asked.

"You kissed me back."

Embarrassed, her cheeks burned. At least there would be no more kisses. She agreed it shouldn't happen again. Because now Serena knew who she was dealing with.

Forget about being baffled and bewildered any longer. Kane was exactly what she'd known him to be the minute she'd met him. Even though his kiss would have knocked her socks off had she been wearing any, he was the epitome of Mr. Wrong.

In every sense of the word.

Forget about being stranded or the bad weather hanging over them or anything else facing her in the wilderness. The most difficult thing she would have to survive was Kane Wiley. She realized something else, too.

For years she had blamed her sister for lacking good judgment about men. Serena touched a finger to her still throbbing lips and finally understood. She really owed Morgan an apology.

In her office, holding on to the phone receiver, Belle listened to the voices chatting in the hallway. She might be shaking inside and this most recent bombshell wasn't helping, but she needed to be strong for her girls. She glanced up.

Callie, wearing a green vinyl apron over her jeans and sweater, stood in the doorway. "Any news yet?"

Not the news Belle had been expecting to hear. "No, darlin'. Don't forget with the three-hour time difference, it's still morning out there. You can't ask a hen to lay an egg before she's ready."

"But we're ready here." Regina sat on the edge of the desk. She didn't have her camera in hand, which told Belle how worried the photographer must be. "I've already eaten three slices of Natalie's banana cake trying to calm my nerves."

"Are you calm?"

"Nope. Just full."

Belle placed the receiver in its cradle. "Charlie sounded hopeful after talking to officials in Idaho."

"Is that who you were talking to?" Callie sat on a chair. "Charlie?"

"No, I haven't heard from him." Well, not in the last half hour. He'd gone home to pack for the trip west. Belle drew in a breath for strength. "I was on the phone with Rupert."

"The poor guy." Regina sighed. "He must be out of his mind with worry."

Callie nodded. "When do Rupert and Charlie fly out there?"

Belle wished she didn't have to answer that question. "Rupert isn't going."

Disappointment flared in Callie's green eyes, something Belle had witnessed a million times before until Jared had entered the florist's life and love had blossomed this past spring. "But he's her boyfriend."

"He has to go." Regina tensed. Belle knew the photographer had learned how important sticking together as a couple was. "Serena's going to need him."

Belle took a calming breath. It didn't help. "Rupert broke up with Serena in April."

"What?" the two women said at the same time. Their mouths remained opened. Their eyes wide.

"But it's November." Callie sounded dumbfounded.

"I knew something was up." Regina's brown eyes

darkened. "But Serena said things were okay and they seemed to be the perfect couple."

"Serena hinted things weren't so great, but she didn't seem that concerned," Callie admitted. "Everything always works out for her."

"That's so true." Belle shivered, feeling as if she'd failed the young designer. Serena looked as if she had it all, and Belle never had to worry about her like some of the other girls. "But appearances aren't always what they seem."

Regina nodded.

Callie pressed her lips together. "I still don't understand why she didn't tell us."

"She must have her reasons," Regina said.

Both the girls sounded hurt and worried. Belle wished she had answers for them. "Remember, this is something Serena needs to tell us on her own, when she's ready, even if we want answers now."

But that didn't stop the pain all three of them felt with Serena gone. It seemed like a piece of Belle's heart was missing along with the designer. She wanted Serena found ASAP.

Regina hopped off the desk. "So if Rupert isn't going to Idaho, who is going to be there for Serena?"

Belle straightened. "I am."

CHAPTER SEVEN

HE NEEDED to have his head examined.

Stomping around in the snow with flurries falling from the sky didn't make a lot of sense to Kane. Neither had kissing Serena. He'd only wanted to kiss her once, not a full-on make-out session, but when she'd pressed against him and kissed him back…

At least gathering firewood gave them time and much-needed space away from each other. He glanced her way. But she was getting a little too far away.

"What are you doing?" he asked.

Serena waved her hot-pink cell phone in the air with a bare hand. "Seeing if I can get a signal on my cell phone."

City girl. He tried for patience. Failed.

"Forget about that and put your gloves back on before you get frostbite." He watched her pull his gloves onto her hands. "Look for fallen trees, branches, anything that looks like it might burn."

"Okay."

Nothing was okay.

Kissing Serena was about the dumbest thing he'd done lately. Sure, he'd enjoyed it. One taste and he wanted to kiss her again. But he couldn't let himself get caught up in the moment again. Putting the moves on a woman who couldn't call a cab and was forced for survival's sake to share his bed violated his personal code of conduct.

Kane brushed the snowflakes from his hair with his sock-covered hands. Maybe the rough landing had shaken up more than the plane.

He shot a sideward glance at Serena, whose feet sunk into the deep snow as she made her way back toward him. "Be careful."

"I'm being careful," she said. "I know how to take care of myself."

Distance, he reminded himself. "And your damn dresses."

"You helped with the dresses." She smiled at him. "In fact, you've helped with everything."

Even distance wasn't proof against her smile. "You don't make it easy."

"I know, but I'm trying to be less…"

"Of a pain in the ass?"

"Hey." She placed her gloved hands on her coat-covered hips. "You said I had a cute ass."

"I did. You do. But you can still be a pain."

"I'm trying to be—"

"Not so self-reliant, independent, stubborn?"

Her mouth quirked. "I was actually going to say more receptive."

To his help? To his kisses? To him? Only the first mattered. He focused on a large branch lying in the snow. "That would make things easier."

He looked at her bright blue eyes and flushed cheeks.

Then again, maybe not.

Kane dragged the branch to the end of the trail leading

back to the cabin. Serena added a smaller branch of her own.

"I'm not used to admitting I can't handle everything out here myself," she said quietly.

"You don't have to." She'd shown glimpses of vulnerability before, but now she didn't seem so afraid to let him know what she was feeling. "Just don't pretend you can."

"I won't."

Kane might find her emotional honesty attractive on one level, but it was also damn inconvenient. Her being vulnerable to him did not mean he would be vulnerable to her. He was not going there. He didn't open himself up to anybody.

And that was the way he was keeping it.

On board a plane bound for Idaho, Belle stared out of the window. The sight of the landscape below, the acres of green fields giving way to tree-covered mountainsides, reminded her of Serena and Kane lost somewhere in the wilderness. Belle closed her eyes for a moment. She needed time to regroup, put her game face on as Callie, resident poker player expert, called it.

Callie, Regina, Natalie, Audra and Julie.

Belle hated leaving them alone, but they had each other. Serena needed someone to be there for her. Still, a few hours ago the tears had fallen like raindrops during a Georgia thunderstorm. The hugs and goodbyes had mingled with their hopes and fears. Belle knew she'd left the shop in strong, capable hands. The five women would keep The Wedding Belles running smoothly until she returned with Serena.

If she returned with Serena…

Belle blew out a puff of air.

"Hang in there." Charlie sat in the aisle seat next to her. "We can't give up hope."

"I'm trying." The compassion in his voice tugged on Belle's heartstrings. "But not knowing anything is hard. Part of me is afraid of what we might find when we get there."

"Sometimes not knowing is better," Charlie admitted. "I remember…"

"What?" She leaned toward him. "Tell me, please."

"Three years ago I got a phone call from Kane telling me his mother, my wife, had suffered a heart attack. He asked me to meet him at the hospital. What he didn't tell me was that the massive coronary had killed her."

"Oh, Charlie." Memories of losing Matthew, tucked deep in her heart, floated to the surface. She remembered the emotions as if they were brand-new and raw, not nine years old. Disbelief, shock and loneliness had rooted themselves in her heart only to be pruned, somewhat, with the passage of time. Belle covered Charlie's hand with her own. "That must have been horrible."

"Not at first. I didn't know," he said. "As I drove to the hospital I worried she might need surgery. That scared me, but the idea of her dying? My mind wouldn't let me go there or I would have fallen apart."

Belle gave his hand a gentle squeeze. "When my husband, Matthew, got sick I knew it was serious. He was older than me, but I believed with all my heart he would recover. I don't know how I could have given him the support, the care he'd needed if I'd thought he was leaving me."

"I had worked everything out in my head by the time I arrived at the hospital. How she would recover, what needed to be done and then Kane told me and…"

"Your world fell apart."

Charlie nodded.

"Mine, too," she said. "At first you have so much to take care of, all the paperwork, the people around you. I felt as if I was living in a fog."

"But the work ends, the people go away and the cloud of shock lifts. And you're left…"

"With nothing." Belle felt a connection, a new bond growing between her and Charlie. "And if you're like me, you're utterly lost, don't know what to do and end up making some really bad decisions."

Surprise filled his eyes. "I thought I was the only one who did that."

"Oh, darlin', I wish that was the case because I made some doozies. A stuffed Thanksgiving turkey had more sense than I did those first two years."

He laughed. So did Belle.

"I'm happy you're with me." His brown eyes darkened to the color of espresso. "No matter what we find out, we'll make it through."

She nodded.

"We'll keep each other from making any doozy mistakes, too," he added. "That's what friends are for."

Friends.

Belle thought she only wanted friendship from Charlie. But sitting here with her hand on top of his, talking with him this way, the word didn't seem nearly enough for her.

Must be the situation, she rationalized. The heightened emotions. The terrifying unknowns. Nothing else made sense.

"Do we have a deal, Belle?"

She pulled her hand from the top of his to shake on his words. "Deal, darlin'."

* * *

That evening, Kane sat across from Serena. She stared at the remnants of their dinner—canned stew, crackers and dried fruit—littering the table. Not exactly gourmet fare.

"Thanks for cooking dinner tonight," he said. "The meal hit the spot after all that wood-gathering."

She placed the wrappers from the crackers on her plate. "That wasn't cooking. I wish the biscuits had turned out."

"Hey, I'm impressed you even attempted biscuits." He leaned back in his chair. "How are your ribs? Sore?"

"A little."

But the rest of Serena's muscles ached, especially her back. Pilates and running, her normal workouts, couldn't compare to gathering firewood in the falling snow.

What she wouldn't give for a massage.

She stretched, happy she'd changed out of her skirt and sweater into her flannel pajama bottoms and a turtleneck. As long as she didn't have to make a late-night run to the outhouse, she'd stay comfy and warm.

Serena glanced around the small cabin, surprisingly content. The crackling wood in the stove kept the temperature comfortable. The propane lighting provided a soft glow. And her companion…

"Dessert?" Kane asked

She would rather have that massage. But dessert was a safer bet than Kane's hands soothing, massaging and making her feel all better. "Let me clean up first."

"No, dessert comes first. Always."

As he rummaged through the food, she studied him. Kane was a contradiction. One minute gruff, the other giving. Serena appreciated his softer, gentler side. To be honest, she kind of liked being taken care of. Not that she would ever tell him that. Or anybody for that matter.

For so long, she'd had to be reliable, successful and independent. She'd dressed to glossy perfection and portrayed the image of a successful wedding dress designer with practiced flair and finesse. But out here in the mountains, in this cozy little cabin with Kane, she could just be herself. She could forget about everyone else's expectations and relax. She could finally be…free.

He extended his arm and offered her a handful of truffles. "Here you go."

She took a heart-shaped chocolate wrapped in cellophane and tied with a lavender ribbon from his hand. "Thanks."

"Just one?"

"This will hit the spot."

"Chocolate always does."

"A man after my own heart." Serena felt his gaze on her. "What?"

"I thought you were a no-chocolate girl."

She unwrapped the piece. "Why?"

"At the bridal show, you didn't eat a chocolate. I figured you were a perpetual dieter who scorned sweets."

"Are you kidding?" She raised the truffle to her nose and sniffed. Heavenly. "All of us Belles, except Natalie, eat wedding cake samples all the time. Chocolate is my favorite."

Serena bit into the crisp dark chocolate shell. The taste exploded in her mouth. Sweet and rich with a hint of bitterness. The creamy inside melted in her mouth. "Mmm."

"That good?"

Nodding, she savored the texture as she took another bite. Oh-so-yummy, but addictive. A little like a kiss from Kane. You wanted more than one taste. But like the handful of truffles he offered her, one was more than enough. Any more wouldn't be smart.

When she was finished, a faint sugary scent remained on her fingertips. At least Kane's kiss hadn't left that on her lips. Serena looked across the table at him. "Aren't you having one?"

"I had two." A devilish grin appeared. "You were too busy enjoying yours to notice."

"Sorry."

"Don't be. I like a woman who can appreciate what's good for her."

"I consider myself a chocolate connoisseur," she said.

"And how do you become a chocolate connoisseur?"

She smiled. "By eating lots and lots of chocolate."

"Then I must be a connoisseur, too." He picked up the carafe he'd brought from the plane and filled their glasses with water he'd melted from snow. "Make sure you drink all of it. You don't want to get dehydrated."

As Serena sipped the warm water, a comforting silence settled between them. They were more like a couple on a vacation in a mountain cabin than two strangers stranded together in the wilderness.

He drank from a mug. She watched him, mesmerized, wishing his lips were touching hers instead. Her cup slipped from her right hand, but she caught it with her left, only spilling a few drops.

Uh-oh. If she weren't careful, she could be the one crashing to the floor. Serena rose and cleared the table.

"You like playing house, don't you?" Kane asked.

As she carried the plates, she glanced his way, suddenly cautious. "I don't play house."

"Never?"

"Never," she admitted, thinking about her sister, Morgan. "I've seen what can go wrong when you play."

"You surprise me, Blondie."

"What do you mean?" Serena asked.

"Underneath all that shine and glamour, you're kind of an old-fashioned girl. Cleaning the cabin. Cooking dinner. Now the dishes."

Old-fashioned? Serena tried to decide whether she was offended by his comment. "It's not old-fashioned to want a clean living space. I grew up doing chores."

"I never did chores." Kane stood. "My mom or the housekeeper did everything."

Serena had been the one to do everything. She'd done her own chores and her sister's, too. Anything she could to make things...perfect.

He took the dishes from her hands. "I've got these."

"I don't mind," she said automatically.

She reached for the dishes, but he wouldn't let go. "I do."

The two held on to the plates as if they were made of fine porcelain, not plastic.

"What are you doing, Blondie?" Kane asked finally. "Trying to earn a gold star on your chore chart?"

Serena blushed. How could he know her so well? "Well, I always did get a lot of gold stars."

"Such a good girl." His lips curved in a teasing, charming, coaxing smile. "Let me do the dishes tonight."

Reluctantly she let go. "Then what will I do?"

"To earn those gold stars?" His eyes gleamed. "I'm sure we can think of something."

The dishes were clean, the fire stoked. All Kane needed to do was crawl into bed. Strike that. Bed brought up the image of rolling around with one sexy blonde who kissed like a dream. Scowling, he rubbed the back of his neck.

"Are you all right?" Serena asked. "You look tense."

He fought the urge to laugh. "I'm fine."

Her pretty blue eyes widened in sympathy. "It's the bed. It's not really big enough for two."

Unless they slept stacked like firewood. And then Kane would guarantee they'd get no sleep at all.

"The bed's fine," he said. "I just need—"

You.

"—a pillow," he finished lamely.

Serena, sitting at the table, perked up. She pulled one of her boxes toward her and searched through it until she pulled out a plump, purple velvet square. "A-ha. One pillow."

Kane raised his eyebrows. "That wasn't in the booth at the show."

"I know. I didn't use it because I couldn't find the slipper."

Kane had no idea what she was talking about. "What slipper?"

"The glass slipper. Cinderella's slipper?"

He continued to stare at her.

She sighed. "You know. Fairy Godmother, Prince Charming, stroke of midnight, happily ever after."

He shook his head. "I don't believe in that stuff."

"Stuff?" she asked.

"Fairy tales and happy endings."

"Why not?"

Thinking about his father and his ex-stepmother left a bitter taste in Kane's mouth. "Happy endings aren't possible because love is transitory. It doesn't last. It can't. As soon as a so-called love is gone the other person is on to the next one."

A beat passed. And another.

The only sounds were the fire in the stove and their breathing.

"It isn't always like that," she said.

This conversation was making him...tired. He headed toward the bed. Maybe she would get the clue he didn't want to talk about this.

"I believe fairy-tale endings exist. That there are people out there who will stand by the one they love through it all, good or bad," she continued, her words full of longing. "Disappointment or failure won't matter because even when things are at their darkest or someone has fallen or whatever horrible thing might happen, the love will remain strong, solid, forever."

He was more moved—and more shaken—than he wanted to admit. "You believe that if you want to."

"What do you believe?" she asked softly.

Looking into her blue eyes, Kane thought he'd like to believe in her.

And that scared him even more than her talk about forever.

He deflected her question with a smile. "I believe in the benefits of a good night's sleep. Toss that pillow over here and let's get some shut-eye."

The next day passed slowly. Snow continued to fall, keeping them trapped inside the cabin. Serena sketched new dress design ideas. Kane worked on an electric box from the plane. By the time evening came and dinner was over, she was ready to do something to work off some energy and take her mind off their plight. Anything.

She glanced at Kane sitting at the table. Okay, not anything.

Serena paced the small confines of the cabin. The smell

from the woodstove seemed to intensify and she longed to feel a cool breeze on her face. What she wouldn't give to smell the ocean or cocoa butter, something tropical.

She'd counted the mice scurrying across the floor—three—and wondered if naming them would be a good idea. She had to do something to keep herself occupied. Boredom might lead her and Kane to do something they shouldn't in order to, well, keep themselves busy.

Serena couldn't think about him that way. Walking away from his father the way he had, told her that he didn't believe in unconditional love. Not that what he believed mattered to her. Still a flicker of disappointment shot through her.

"Bored?" he asked.

"A little."

"Cabin fever is no fun," Kane said.

That was better than another kind of fever. She gulped.

"I'm sure we can think of something to do."

She was sure they could. That's what worried her. Outside, a wolf howled somewhere in the distance.

"I have a game for couples to know each other better somewhere," she suggested. "But we're not a couple."

"No, but we are sleeping together."

Serena glared at him.

He laughed. "Don't worry, you're still the kind of girl a guy would want to take home to meet the parents. My father thinks you're great."

She smiled. "Your dad is so sweet."

"He has his moments." Kane got this faraway look in his eyes when he talked about Charlie that suggested he wasn't as indifferent to his dad as he pretended.

The wolf howled again, the lonely cry cutting through the cold night air.

"What about your mom?" she asked, intrigued enough to want to know more about Kane.

"If my mom were still here, she would like you," Kane said, his voice full of warmth.

Serena sat across from him. "What was she like?"

"She was the best and had so much love to give." A soft smile formed on his lips. "The two of you…you have a lot in common. She was into clothes, loved to sew and subscribed to a stack of fashion magazines. My mom would have talked your ear off about what you do and she would have invited you shopping."

Kane's tone spoke of a deep love for his mother. His words wrapped around Serena like an old quilt, comfy and warm and stitched with affection. "She sounds wonderful."

"She was."

The two simple words spoke volumes when coupled with the emotion—the love—in his eyes. And that was when Serena realized Kane Wiley wasn't totally the loner, the free spirit he claimed to be. She had seen his passion with his flying and experienced it with his kiss. She'd also realized that he felt loss deeply. Buried inside had to be a man with a streak of romance, longing for commitment. If only she could get to see that side of him…

"Tell me what your parents would think if you brought me home to meet them."

"They would not like you at all."

He laughed.

Oh, no. Had she said that out loud? Her cheeks burned. "It's just my parents have a pretty well-defined view of who would make an acceptable…partner for their daughters. My parents are overachievers. That's what they raised my sister, Morgan, and me to be."

"Looks like they succeeded."

With me at least. "They want us to be happy."

"Happiness to them is having you marry some guy in a suit with a solid background, a stable job and a good income with the potential for more so you will have whatever you want or need."

"Pretty much."

"You want the same thing?"

His words hung in the air, as if they floated in front of her like a movie special effect. *You want the same thing?* She thought about what she wanted most of all. She wanted her plans to be realized. She wanted to make people happy. She wanted…

An answer formed deep inside of her and burst to the surface. "I want true love."

"Ah, the fairy tale again." He studied her. "You've got everything figured out."

She raised her chin. "I've got a plan."

"Let's hear it."

"Well, once I find Mr. Right, we date for a year, are engaged for a year, get married, buy a house, wait another year before we get pregnant and then we have a baby."

Kane laughed. "I don't know whether to be impressed at your knowing what you want or worried for the poor guy you choose."

Her cheeks felt warm. "Well, I'm a planner."

"Nothing wrong with that except sometimes plans don't work out the way you think they will."

"Tell me about it." Serena sighed. Kane was so easy to talk to. She'd been more up-front and honest with him, whom she'd known—and fought with—for only a couple of days, than with the women she'd known and worked with for years. "I'm missing the most important thing in my plan. Mr. Right."

"Hey—" he reached across the table and touched the corner of her mouth with his fingertip "—smile, Blondie. He's out there."

"You think?" She cringed at the insecurity in those two words.

"I know," Kane reassured. "Think positively."

She felt anything but positive. "He's out there. Somewhere."

"Absolutely. You'll find him."

Serena nodded once and stared down at the table.

"Look." He lifted her chin with his finger. "I'm about as far away from Mr. Right as you would want, but if you'd like, I could be your Mr. Right Now."

CHAPTER EIGHT

MR. RIGHT NOW.

Kane shook his head in self-disgust. What was he thinking?

Like Miss-Seeking-Happily-Ever-After-Tied-Up-In-A-Neat-Little-Bow would settle for a torrid three-day or less affair with a no-strings flyboy.

Not that he didn't like the idea. He liked it a lot. He liked her a lot.

Which was part of the problem.

She'd be a lot easier to resist if she were the spoiled ice princess he'd pegged her as at their first meeting.

The wolf howled again. Louder this time. Closer.

Serena's forehead wrinkled. Her mouth tightened.

Uh-oh. He rose from the table and snuck a peek out of the window. The darkness prevented him from seeing anything. "The howl is likely a neighbor's dog barking. The wolf won't bother us."

Or shouldn't under normal circumstances. But with their luck…

The howl turned into howls.

Right on cue. Kane shook his head, but he shouldn't have been surprised.

Turning slightly, Serena craned her neck to peer at the door. "That sounds like more than one wolf."

"Probably just a family," he said nonchalantly, wanting to take the wariness in her voice away. "A dad, mom, pups."

"You mean a pack."

The howling continued. Intensified. He heard shuffling outside. Something scratched at the door.

A layer of tension filled the cabin. The lighting seemed to dim. Serena's lower lip quivered. Not a lot, but enough so he noticed. She looked stiff, tight, scared. Maybe he'd mistaken tension for fear.

Kane didn't feel like smiling at the moment, but forced one anyway. "We're inside. They're outside. No worries."

"No worries," Serena repeated, but kept her head turned and her eyes focused on the door. If she kept that position for any length of time, she would add twisted neck to her injuries.

Not on his watch.

Kane carried his chair over and wedged the top under the door handle. "Wolves usually stay away from humans. I've never known a wolf to open a door, but just in case these Idaho ones know any special tricks, the chair will add a little insurance."

As she turned to face him, her tense shoulders relaxed. "Thanks."

He blew out a puff of air. Now what? "So…"

"So what does a 'Mr. Right Now' do?"

Damn. Kane thought he'd gotten away with that one scot-free. He was trying to resist temptation, but if temptation—or Serena—threw itself in his lap… "Whatever you want him to do."

The howling continued, but Serena didn't glance back.

She stood instead. Her gaze, a mix of anticipation and alarm in her eyes, met his. "Would you hold me?"

In a New York minute. The vulnerable look on her face and the sexy way she looked in her pajamas smacked him right in the gut. He sat on her chair and pulled Serena onto his lap. "How's this?"

"Nice."

Nice didn't begin to describe how good holding her on his lap felt. More like perfect.

Wolves howled outside. Wind blew through the trees and rattled the windows. Wood burned in the stove, crackling and popping, the now familiar scent of smoke lofting in the air.

Kane still felt as if nothing else existed. Nothing else mattered. He wrapped his arms around her. Soft and warm and all his. Well, for as long as she allowed.

"Thank you," she murmured.

He should be thanking her. And the wolves. "No problem."

It wasn't.

Not now.

Ask him again in a few minutes.

"It's probably silly to be frightened of a few overgrown dogs," she said. "I think the wolves were the final straw after everything that's happened. I'm not very good at this adventure stuff."

He ran his finger along her jaw to her chin. Soft with a determined edge. Like the woman herself. "Being out here alone is nothing like being back in Boston."

She smiled. "But I'm not alone. I have you."

Kane swallowed. "For now."

He was not in this for the long haul. One of them had to remember that.

She leaned back, giving him the chance to nuzzle his nose against her hair. The scent of strawberries, sweet and fresh and juicy, filled his nostrils. The smell reminded him of spring, flowers blooming and sunny days, not a day in early November with drifting snow outside as far as the eye could see. He took another sniff. Her lotion? Or just Serena?

The answer didn't matter.

Not with her on his lap in his arms cuddling against him as if she belonged there. His blood boiled, pounding through his veins with purpose and direction. That could be embarrassing. He needed to think cool thoughts. Arctic thoughts might work best.

"You want to know something?" Serena asked.

Anything to stop thinking about her and the way she smelled. "What?"

"Even though I feel out of sorts tonight, I'd rather be here than in Boston."

Her words headed straight to his heart, crashing through his defense system with their sincerity. "Me, too."

And if Kane were smart, he would end this right now. The situation had *bad news* written all over it. She wasn't looking for something temporary. He wasn't looking for something permanent. Someone was going to get hurt.

Not hurt.

He…respected Serena too much to hurt her, to take advantage of her trust and the situation.

All Kane wanted to do was hold her. Well, not all. But it would do. It had to.

He pulled her closer, careful of her ribs, mindful of where he placed his hands. Her heartbeat drummed against him, the increasing tempo matching his own.

Another noise sounded outside the door. Wind, wolf? Hard to tell.

Serena turned, her face right next to his. Her warm breath fanned his cheek. Big blue eyes stared deep into his, probing and searching. Attraction buzzed between them.

Kane's self-control slipped a notch. Okay, two.

She'd asked him to hold her. She'd wanted comfort, but the flash of desire in her eyes and her parted lips told him she also wanted…

"Kiss me," she whispered. "Please."

She wasn't going to have to ask twice.

Brushing his lips over hers, Kane wanted to soothe her. Calm and reassure her, too. He wanted his kiss to make her feel special, cherished and adored. The way a woman should always feel.

This kiss was different, sweeter and softer than their ones yesterday, but just as good. With each passing moment, he struggled to keep the kiss gentle and not allow his growing desire to take over. Hard to do when she was in his arms and kissing him. Talk about heaven on earth.

It couldn't get much better than this.

She leaned into him, into the kiss, pressing her lips against his. Her tongue sought, found, danced with his.

So much for tenderness.

His blood pressure spiraled. Logical thought disappeared. Common sense fled.

There was only here and now.

Only Serena.

The realization should have bothered him more than it did, but Kane didn't care. Right now this…she…was all that mattered. He ran his hands through her hair, the short strands sifting through his fingers.

Pulling her closer, he deepened the kiss. She tasted like chocolate. Expensive and rich and filling. He wanted another taste. And another.

As his tongue explored her mouth, she moaned. The husky sound excited him, bringing a twinge to his groin.

Her fingertips ran along the muscles on his back. Rubbing, kneading, exploring. Her eagerness pleased him. Turned him on. Made him want more.

Want her.

Want all of her.

Damn. This was getting out of control. Who was he kidding? The situation was reaching breaking point.

Kane had to stop kissing her. Now.

Before the kisses turned into something more. He couldn't do that to Serena even if she were the one who asked for the kiss. She needed more than he was willing to give her. She wanted a man who would commit. Just like Amber and every other woman he'd known. He wasn't that man.

He kissed Serena, soaking up the taste of her for one last time and pulled away. Her breathing ragged, she looked at him with those big eyes, eyes clouded with desire for him, and full lips, lips bruised and swollen from kissing him. He'd never seen a woman look more beautiful or sexier.

Kane struggled to breathe.

"Wow." She scooted off his lap and stood next to the table. "I'm not sure what to say."

"Thank you would suffice."

She smiled shyly. "Thank you."

"Anytime. I mean, if you want something or need…"

"I know what you mean, Kane."

That made one of them because he hadn't a clue.

"What now?" Serena asked.

Oh, he had lots of ideas, but none of them would be good for her. Or, come to think of it, him. "Sleep."

"Sleep?" She sounded a little confused.

That made two of them.

Why did she have to be so sweet, so pretty, so damn sexy? Why did she want to find true love instead of hot sex? Why couldn't they…?

"Maybe I should sleep on the floor," he said. "On blankets."

"You want to sleep on the floor?" she asked, her voice as soft as a snowflake. "Is that really what you want to do?"

Forget about what he wanted to do. That would only make things worse. "It's probably a good idea tonight. Taking this physical stuff any further—"

"Wouldn't be smart," she finished for him. "But I hate for you to sleep on the floor. What if we were to agree to be on our best behavior, a gentleman and a gentlewoman, and made sure nothing else happened?"

"Would you feel comfortable enough with that?" he asked.

She nodded. "I trust you, Kane."

Her words pierced his heart like an arrow shot at the bull's-eye. Direct hit.

He nearly staggered back a step.

But his heart didn't hurt. It wanted…more.

That meant one thing. Serena was getting too close. Kane knew exactly what he had to do or rather what he couldn't do. No more cuddling, no more kisses and no more Mr. Right Now.

Tempted or not, his heart was off-limits. And he wasn't about to change that.

"We have pinpointed a possible location," on-scene Incident Commander Logan Michaels explained to Charlie and Belle at a mobile command post in the Clearwater

National Forest. He pointed to a large topographical map with red marks and circles drawn on it. "The weather has the air search grounded again, but a search and rescue team is riding to Gold Meadows on horseback. In a situation like this, we put calls out for assistance. County and state lines don't matter much. We've got a unit from Missoula, Montana, waiting to assist with the evacuation and another group on standby."

Excitement surged through Belle. "Wonderful news to start the day."

She hugged Charlie, who spun her around as if she were sixteen not sixty-five. Heat rushed up her cheeks.

He placed her on her feet. "Sorry about that."

"No need to apologize." The tingles in Belle's stomach actually felt good. "I didn't mind."

And that was the truth. She liked having someone to lean on after so long.

Charlie's eye-reaching grin filled Belle with surprising joy.

"How did you pinpoint them?" he asked.

"Cell phone technology," Logan said. "A local cellular company found pings from one of the phones."

One. At least one of them was alive. Belle muttered a silent prayer. She hated being greedy, but one of them surviving wasn't enough.

Charlie looked at her. His mouth tight. His jaw set.

Belle didn't know him well, but she knew enough about him to know the question he wanted answered. A question he wasn't capable of asking himself. "Do you know whose cell phone had been turned on? Kane's or Serena's?"

"Serena's," Logan answered.

A shadow crossed Charlie's face. Belle reached for him, linking her hand with his. "That doesn't mean—"

"I know."

"Kane could be using the phone," she said. "We don't know enough to make any assumptions."

"Belle is correct, Charlie," Logan said. "Your concern is understandable given the circumstances, but there are so many unknowns we just don't know. What you can count on is the experience and expertise of the SAR unit out there searching for Kane and Serena."

"SAR?" Belle asked, thinking of the Asian disease from a few years ago.

"Search and Rescue," Logan explained. "You won't find a better group of men and women. One of the best SAR experts in the country is out there, too. Jake Porter. He's from Oregon Mountain Search and Rescue and was training our unit this past weekend. When the call came in on Sunday, he decided to stay on and join the team in the field."

Belle forced a smile. "Well, you can't ask for more than that, can you, darlin'?"

The strain on Charlie's face eased. "I guess you can't. We appreciate your efforts, Logan. And everyone out there in the cold snowy weather looking for Kane and Serena."

"You're welcome." Logan pointed to a map. "Just so you know, Gold Meadows has been used in the past as a helicopter landing site while fighting forest fires. There's also a small cabin there with provisions, light and heat."

"More good news," Belle said.

"It could be. I will let you know when I hear more news," Logan said. "I also want to let you know the media has picked up the story. You may be asked for a statement. It's your choice if you do or don't. The sheriff's office has a public relations liaison who will work with you."

"Thank you." Belle and Charlie spoke at the same time.

His gaze caught hers. His brown eyes seemed to see right inside her, straight to her heart. Warmth flooded through her like a sip of hot cocoa with a dash of Peppermint Schnapps mixed in. The reaction was unexpected, but surprisingly not unwelcome.

The realization set off about a zillion warning bells in her head. She'd had her chance at the love of a lifetime with her beloved Matthew. She didn't want a boyfriend let alone something serious.

But still Belle found herself sneaking a peek at the handsome and charming Charlie.

The next morning, Serena woke feeling rested and warm as if she were waking in her own bed at home, not a rustic little cabin in the woods. Kane lay with his chest against her back, his arm draped over her hip and his legs entwined with hers.

She felt his breath on her neck. The warm puffs of air comforted her. The same way his snores had during the night.

She'd held up her end of the bargain and so had he. Kane had been the perfect gentleman, as promised. Just as she knew he would be. But that hadn't made things any easier.

She touched her lips. Slightly swollen as if she'd used a plumping lipstick. But these lips were strictly the result of Kane, not some cosmetic recipe.

Kiss me, please.

Serena couldn't believe she'd said those words. She wished she could blame her lapse on fear over the wolves and a sudden realization that they were truly lost, but she knew better. Being held had eased her worry, but ignited a spark. One that didn't want to be doused.

She'd wanted to be kissed. She'd needed to be kissed.
By him.

Only him.

Kane had delivered. His kisses made her feel safe,
secure and accepted. Without her usual gloss of manners
and accomplishments, without the armor of designer
clothing, without styling gel and concealer, he made her
feel beautiful. Sexy. Herself.

She could be herself and that was enough. Freeing.

Serena glanced at him, her heart filling with satisfaction. She couldn't forget this wasn't real. They were
playing house—make that cabin—with no one else around
except a pack of wolves, birds and an occasional mouse
scampering across the floor. What happened here would
never have happened back home. It couldn't.

Still the experience only reaffirmed what she wanted in
life. Serena was tired of living up to other people's expectations and demands. She wanted a man who would love
her for herself. Without strings. Without conditions. She
wanted to find what she'd found temporarily in Kane's
arms.

If only it could be him…

No. She couldn't allow herself to even daydream about
that. Kane Wiley could never be her Mr. Right. He'd
admitted that himself.

But still her heart wanted him.

Not going to happen.

All Serena had to do was push emotion aside and look at
the situation logically. Look at Kane that way, too. Mentally
she composed a list of everything wrong with him:

1. Does not love unconditionally
2. Cannot forgive

3. No longer believes in happily ever after
4. Values freedom more than anything including relationships
5. Kisses so well that reasons 1-4 don't matter

Darn him.

Not a problem. In spite of number five, she had learned from Morgan's mistakes and would not repeat them herself.

Serena pulled her leg away from his and crawled off the bed quietly. The wood floor was cold beneath her socked feet. She padded to the window. No sight of any wolves, but snow fell. Disappointment settled in the bottom of her tummy. Snow meant another day and night in the cabin. At least another twenty-four tempting hours with Kane.

Don't think about that.

Instead Serena got busy. She added wood to the stove to keep the cabin warm, dressed in her heaviest skirt and reminded herself to always pack warm clothes when traveling. She needed to use the outhouse, but hesitated at the door. What if the wolves were still out there? She opened the door slowly. Pawprints were everywhere.

"Going somewhere, Blondie?"

The rich sound of his voice sent the butterflies in her tummy flapping their wings. Those were going to have to stop right now. "I was seeing if the wolves were still out there."

"Are they?" he asked.

Feeling tongue-tied, she shrugged.

What was going on? She was Serena James, the hottest new name in wedding dress design. She had a great job, her own flat. She always knew the right thing to say whether talking with a friend or giving a sound bite. She was capable, successful and reliable. But Kane made her feel like she was back in junior high school, thin and awkward-looking, standing against the wall by herself, waiting to be asked to dance at the ball.

"Want to wear a pair of my pants?" he asked.

"I don't think they'd fit but if they did I'd have to stop eating."

A corner of his mouth turned up. "I'm sure with your vast fashion expertise you could figure out how to keep my pants on you."

"Thanks, but this skirt is wool." She remembered how intimate wearing his shirt the first night had felt. His pants might be worse. No more intimacy allowed!

"Suit yourself." He grabbed a pair of jeans from his bag. "I'm going to change clothes then I can make sure there aren't any more four-footed visitors hanging around outside."

Serena looked out of the window at the falling snow. She felt as if she were falling, too, and didn't like the feeling one bit. The only way to get what she wanted was to be in control. She'd figured that out years ago.

As the teeth of a zipper being undone filled the quiet cabin, a flare of heat burst through her. She grimaced at her reaction. So much for self-control.

She didn't understand why Kane had such an effect on her, but somehow she had to learn how to control her reactions. No way was she going to do anything with Mr. Wrong she might regret.

Even if she might like it.

During breakfast, Kane kept the topics of conversation light—weather, food and sports teams. Anything to distance himself from her because the first thing he'd wanted to do when he woke up and saw Serena was kiss her. So much for off-limits.

Time to get serious.

"I'm going to hike out to the plane," he said.

"I'll come with you."

"No." The word came out harsher than he intended. "Stay here and doodle in your book."

"Do you mean this book?" She pulled a notebook out of her bag. "This is a sketch pad. I use it to come up with design ideas."

"Then stay here and work." He ignored the hurt in her eyes. He couldn't afford to care. "It's better than you getting cold."

"I don't melt in the cold."

A knock sounded on the door.

Serena looked at him.

Another knock.

"I don't think it's the wolves." He sprang out of his chair and opened the door. Five people stood outside. The first four wore matching green jackets. The fifth, hanging back a ways, wore a red and black jacket. Kane smiled. "We are so glad to see you."

"I'm Ray Massey," the first in green, a man in his early forties, said. "With the Idaho County Sheriff's Posse."

"Kane Wiley." He motioned behind him. "This is Serena James. Come in."

The team entered the cabin, making the space even more crowded.

"Are either of you injured?" Ray asked.

"Serena has a cut on her head and bruised ribs."

"We all are Wilderness First Responders and a couple of us are EMTs, too," Ray said to her. "Can we examine you?"

"That's fine," she said.

"Freeman and Porter," Ray ordered.

Freeman wore a heavy green jacket with the words *Sheriff's Posse* written in black on the back. Porter wore a black and red jacket with the initials *OMSAR* written in white on the front and *rescue* on the sleeves.

"Nice setup. Warm. Dry." Ray looked around. "Good job."

"Good job getting to us," Kane said. "How'd you find us?"

"Cell phone pings."

Serena's little pink phone. He'd told her to put the damn thing away. Good thing she hadn't listened to him. He admired her resourcefulness and stubbornness, but felt like an idiot for not pulling out his own cell phone.

Kane looked over at her, feeling a burst of protectiveness when he saw the two men examining her bare stomach. The one in green knelt in front of her while the one in red and black stood.

"Don't worry," Freeman said to Serena. "I've done this before."

"On a dummy," one of his team members teased.

"Nah, don't you remember?" another team member said. "He got his junior certification last week."

Serena laughed, the tension evaporating from her shoulders.

"You're in good hands, miss," Ray said. "Freeman's new at this, but Porter is from Oregon Mountain Search and Rescue. He knows exactly what he's doing."

She looked up at Porter. "I've seen those mountain rescues in Oregon on the news. I'm sure I'm in good hands."

"Hey," Freeman said. "We have mountains in Idaho, too."

Porter winked. "You've got foothills here, kid."

All three laughed.

Serena caught Kane staring at her. "What?"

He took a deep breath. It didn't stop the strange feeling in his stomach. "Good job, Blondie. You and that hot-pink phone of yours got us rescued."

"Really?"

Ray nodded. "The cell phone company used your pings to determine your location."

"That's great." Her eyes twinkled. "Guess I contributed something to this adventure after all."

"You contributed a lot more than that, Serena." As a thousand-watt smile lit up her face, Kane's mouth went dry. And that was when he knew. Oh, maybe he'd already figured it out but hadn't admitted to himself. Now he had no doubt. She'd gotten under his skin somehow and wormed her way into his heart.

Good thing they were getting out of here.

"Her head is healing nicely with the two butterfly bandages. No sign of infection. No evidence of a concussion," Freeman said to Ray. "Her ribs are sore. Bruised, but she should have an X-ray to rule out any kind of fracture. She can get out on her own."

"Porter?" Ray asked. "How'd the newbie do?"

"The newbie did fine," Porter said. "Good assessment, kid."

"Let's get going, before the snow really starts falling." Ray clapped his hands. "We've got clothes for you to change into. We may have to do something about those boots though, miss. Those heels might cause some problems."

"You'd be surprised what she can do in them," Kane mumbled.

Serena shot him a warning look. "That's fine, Ray."

"We'll try to save them if we can. We'll line your feet in plastic bags to keep them dry," Ray continued, smiling at her. All of the rescue team seemed to be smiling at her. Not that Kane blamed them. She was beautiful. "We're on horseback so we can pack out as much as we can. The rest will have to wait until spring."

"I don't need anything but my purse and the dress bags," she said, the competent, strong-willed dress designer re-emerging.

"Dress bags?" Ray asked.

"Those bulky white things hanging on the bunk," Kane answered. "And trust me, she won't leave the cabin without them."

CHAPTER NINE

"WE'RE almost there, Serena." Jake Porter encouraged her along the snow-covered trail as they traveled on horseback. The way he had for hours. "Warm enough?"

"Toasty and dry in these clothes you guys loaned me." She appreciated his humor and upbeat attitude, not to mention his killer smile and blue eyes, but she was ready to get there. Wherever "there" might be. "Thanks."

Kane rode thirty yards behind her with one of the wedding dress bags. The others were spread among the rescuers. She smiled at him.

He smiled back and gave her the thumbs-up sign. He was happy. They were on their way back to civilization. She was safe. So why did it feel as if she were riding to her doom?

Serena concentrated on what was in front of her. The rows of trees stood like sentry guards on the side of the trail. As they came to a swinging bridge over the Lochsa River, the hair on the back of her neck stood up. She gripped the reins tightly. But the horse knew what to do and crossed without incident. They continued up the trail another two hundred yards until they reached...a trail-head. Her breath caught in her throat.

"Welcome to Eagle Mountain Trailhead." Ray, who led the group, glanced back and grinned.

"We're here?" she asked.

"I told you we were close," Jake said.

"I thought you were trying to keep me motivated."

He grinned. "That, too."

"You guys did a good job." A bittersweet relief washed over her. Now she could go home. She'd also have to say goodbye to Kane. Her chest tightened. "Thank you."

Serena emerged from the path and saw trucks, SUVs, police cars and four media vans with satellite dishes crammed into the gravel pullout. A uniformed official helped her off the horse.

"Your boyfriend will be out soon," Ray said, standing by her side.

"My boyfriend? No, he's my—" what was he? "—my pilot."

Ray looked from Serena to Kane, glowering as he rode from the trail, and gave a masculine-sounding grunt. "Right."

A few people, reporters, barked questions at her. Cameras flashed. She crossed her arms over her chest.

"Ignore them," Ray advised, a protective arm around her back. "You can decide later if you want to talk to the media."

She inhaled deeply, the cold, icy air stinging her lungs. "Why are they here?"

"The two of you made headlines," he explained.

Kane stood next to them. She fought the urge to scoot closer to him. "Slow news day, huh?" he asked.

"You know it." Ray laughed. "Come on, let's get you guys inside the trailer."

Serena hesitated. Life hadn't stopped with their disappearance. Only their lives. Now everything would probably change back once she stepped inside the trailer. She looked at Kane, hoping for some sort of sign things would stay the same, the way they had been at the cabin. The odds were low. The chances were slim, but still she hoped.

"Ready, Serena?" he said.

Serena, not Blondie.

Too late. She felt like a cement block had taken the place of her heart. Things had already changed.

Four microphones, each with a different channel—eight, thirteen, seventeen and twenty-three—and four digital voice recorders sat on the table in front of Kane. Four cameras were pointed in their direction. Talk about overkill. One would have been too many.

Kane leaned back in his chair at the community medical center in Missoula where they'd been taken for checkups after being debriefed and returning their borrowed winter gear. All he wanted was for this press conference about their non-newsworthy experience to end.

"Well, I couldn't exactly wear one of the wedding dresses," Serena answered yet another stupid question.

The audience, consisting of a handful of journalists, four television reporters and two high school students, laughed. But the entire White House Press Corps could have been present and the result would have been the same. In her borrowed surgical scrubs and hair that hadn't been washed in days, she had captivated the media. Kane, too. He forced himself not to stare. It wasn't easy. She shone, tossing out witty sound bites like Halloween candy.

Pride welled in him. She'd been through so much yet she'd demonstrated such grace and grit in dealing with everything today. Everything since Sunday. Saying good-bye wasn't going to be fun, even though it had to be done.

"Though Kane suggested I should," Serena added.

Her confidence bloomed under the spotlight. He'd seen the same thing at the bridal show. Super Serena. But Kane missed the woman he'd gotten to know at the cabin. He hadn't seen a glimpse of her since they'd stepped in the trailer earlier. Actually since they'd left the cabin with the rescue team. Where had she gone?

"Were you scared when you had to land on a snow-covered meadow, Kane?" a reporter in the second row asked.

A "yes" or a "no" answer wasn't going to satisfy the perched vultures. They would keep asking questions until they got the quote they wanted. Kane didn't want to waste time. He decided to take a page out of Serena's playbook and give the reporters what they wanted.

"There can be an element of fear whenever something goes wrong in the cockpit. But you're so busy reacting that emotions take a back seat. At least until you realize the plane is barreling toward a dense forest of trees and there's nothing you can do to stop it. Then, yeah, you're scared."

"Were you scared, Serena?" the same reporter asked.

"I was terrified. I kept praying Kane was as good a pilot as he said he was." She glanced sideways at him and smiled. "Turns out he was."

Her compliment made him feel so good. He sat straighter, as if showing people she was right, realized what he'd done and leaned back again.

"How would you describe your relationship with each other after your ordeal together?" a woman in the back yelled.

He thought about sleeping with his chest pressed

against her back. The next day when he'd kissed her for the first time and she'd surprised him by kissing back. Then last night when she'd sat on his lap and asked him to kiss her. His temperature jumped ten degrees.

"Want to take this one?" Serena asked, apprehension clear in her eyes.

He remembered her pseudo-boyfriend, her insecurity and her need to project a positive image. She might be Super Serena, but she wanted help with the question. He wasn't about to turn her down. Kane nodded.

"First, I'd like to clarify something," he said. "Ordeal doesn't exactly describe what we went through. There were no hysterics. We had little choice where we landed, but we kept our cool. We had what we needed to be comfortable—a warm place to stay, water to drink and food to eat. Serena might look like a city girl, but she knew how to survive in the wilderness. She kept trying to get a signal on her cell phone and that led to our rescue. The swift action of the search and rescue team got us out of the wilderness area in hours. Wouldn't you agree, Serena?"

"It was actually kind of fun. Well, except the night a pack of wolves paid us a visit."

"You're lucky they only dropped by one night." The on-site incident commander, Logan Michaels, sat to Kane's left and drank coffee as if his life depended on caffeine to stay awake. No doubt he hadn't slept in a while. "Those wolves and their incessant howling drove out a team of field researchers a couple of years ago."

"Then it's a good thing we were found before the wolves came back." As Kane spoke, reporters scribbled notes. "As for your question, Serena James started out as a passenger, a wedding dress designer from Boston. But she's so much more than what she does for a living. Serena never gave up or gave in, even when she was a little worried. She deserves full credit for making our location known to authorities so we could be found. I'm proud to call her my—" *girlfriend* "—my friend."

"Thanks, Kane." Her gaze, full of gratitude and warmth, met his. "I consider you my friend, too."

He didn't want to be her friend, damn it. But anything else—

"What do you plan on doing now?" another reporter asked.

Serena turned her attention back to the crowd. "I'm flying to Boston and getting right back to work with The Wedding Belles."

"What about you, Kane?" the same reporter asked.

He thought about all he'd lost in Gold Meadows—his home, his livelihood, his heart. No, he'd almost lost that, but not quite. The other things, however…

"I need to talk to the insurance company and the Forest Service about my plane and to someone in Seattle about the contaminated fuel. That will probably occupy my time for a while."

And a good thing.

He needed something to think about so he could put Serena James out of his mind. Because that's exactly where she belonged, even if his heart didn't agree.

"We can do this tomorrow, darlin'." Belle's eyes clouded with concern. "You look tired."

Tired didn't begin to describe how Serena felt. She wasn't sure whether the ride out or the press conference or pretending she and Kane were just friends had been more taxing, but she couldn't crawl between the sheets of the motel bed yet. "I need to take care of this."

She opened the closet door to where six no-longer-white dress bags hung. The small space smelled like the cabin. Serena fought the rush of memories of her and Kane. She'd just said goodbye to him an hour ago, but it seemed like days. "The smoke from the woodstove seeped into the bags. I hope it's the bags, not the dresses. Otherwise…"

"Don't borrow worry." Belle held on to six new dress bags a local bridal store had sold her to transport the dresses back to Boston tomorrow. "Trust me on this one."

"I will." Serena fought the tears stinging her eyes. She'd been battling an internal struggle and felt guilty. So many people had been worried. So many people endured the cold, snowy weather to look for them. But Serena wished she were still at the cabin with Kane, where she could just be herself. "Having you here means so much. I don't know what I would have done if I'd walked into that trailer and only seen strangers."

"You had Kane with you."

Not really. "It's not the same as having someone you love there. Thank you for coming all this way to be with me."

Belle set the bags on the bed. She enveloped Serena in one of her trademark hugs. "I'm glad to be here, darlin'."

The scent of Belle's perfume comforted Serena like the smell of her favorite chocolate cake. Her friends who worked at The Wedding Belles were what really mattered. What happened at the cabin had been simply…a dream.

And yet, she'd felt more real, more alive, more herself there. Kane's praise about her courage and uncomplaining attitude had been real, too. Not like a dream at all.

"I kept your parents updated."

"Thanks." And then it hit Serena. If Belle had called her

parents, she had probably called… "Did you talk to anyone else?"

"Yes."

Rupert. The air evaporated from Serena's lungs. She struggled to breathe.

"Let's not worry about that now," Belle said. "We'll have plenty of time to talk about things later. Once you're rested and back home. Okay?"

Serena swallowed around the snowball-size lump in her throat as she felt herself drifting back to the way she'd been before the time in the cabin. Kane would never have let her get away with an evasion like that. "Thank you again."

"Anytime, darlin'."

Serena unzipped the first bag with a hesitant hand. All the dress bags looked alike. She had no idea which gown was inside which bag. Each catch of the zipper felt like a countdown to the moment of truth. Afraid to look, she closed her eyes and pushed the bag off and away.

Belle released a rebel yell.

Serena's eyelids sprang open. She stared at a perfectly white wedding dress made of chiffon with crystals sprayed across the gown. "Thank goodness."

"It looks perfect."

She studied the gown as if inspecting a perfect jewel for a flaw. She left no thread unexamined, but found no problems. Oh, the dress was a little crushed and a lot wrinkled, but nothing steaming or a careful pressing wouldn't fix.

"It is perfect." Serena sniffed the fabric. "And no smoke smell, either. I don't believe it."

Belle grinned. "Believe it."

Serena put the gown into a new bag and zipped it up.

"On to the next one."

She unzipped the bag. Not even halfway down, she stopped.

Belle grimaced. "That's not just smoke I smell."

"Mildew maybe."

"Let's see how bad it is." Belle gasped when the dress came out of the bag. "It's…"

"Ruined." Tears prickled Serena's eyes seeing the water and dirt spots on the diamond-white satin with a champagne tulle lace overlay. Small holes had destroyed the Alencon lace around the neckline. Had a mouse gotten inside somehow? "At least it's a sample dress from the new collection, not a custom gown."

Like Callie's dress.

Don't borrow worry.

Easier said than done.

With a heavy heart, she continued on. To her surprise, the next two dresses came out fine. One, a sleeveless silk with a cutaway skirt, and the other, a satin with embellished lace on the bodice and sleeves. Wrinkled, but fresh smelling. Neither, however, was Callie's dress.

When Serena came to the next dress bag, her heart pounded in her ears. She was almost afraid to go on. Unzipping the next bag, she recognized the beading on the bodice.

Her hand froze. "This is Callie's dress."

Belle sucked in a breath.

The zipper went down three more inches and Serena's heart plummeted. The air whooshed from her lungs. She sagged against the door frame.

"What is it?" Belle asked.

"Callie's dress—" Serena's voice cracked "—it's ruined."

As she pulled the dress bag away, a mouse fell out. Belle screeched and jumped away. Serena was too dejected to care.

She stared at what had once been her most exquisite creation. A strapless A-line corset-back gown with delustered satin alternating with rows of scalloped lace giving the dress a fairy-tale feel yet a strong, contemporary silhouette. Swarovski crystals, bugle beads and seed beads embellished the bodice. The dress had been designed with Callie in mind, but now…

Forget calling what remained a wedding gown. The wet, dirty, smelly and holey dress looked like a farce, a bad joke gone too far. It wasn't fair.

Serena fought back the tears. She had to be strong and hold herself together. She needed to show Belle she could handle this. But inside, she trembled, a potent combination of failure and disappointment grabbing hold of her. She longed to have Kane here, for him to tell her everything would be okay, for him to help her fix this the way he had everything else since landing in the meadow.

"You're going to have to use one of the gowns you have back at the studio for her," Belle said calmly.

"No." Serena raised her chin. "I promised Callie I would take care of her dress. I owe her a one-of-a-kind creation and that's what she'll have."

"Callie's wedding is less than two weeks away," Belle said. "You've already lost this week and still have other obligations to meet, darlin'."

"Don't worry about a thing. I can do this."

And Serena would.

As fingers of sunrise broke over the mountains to the east, Serena sat in a corner booth at the coffee shop attached to the motel in Missoula, Montana. She warmed her cold hands on a steaming cup of coffee.

"Mind if I join you?"

The familiar male voice brought a sensation of pleasure rippling through her. Kane. She'd missed him so much already, which made no sense. She'd only spent a night away from him, but what a night.

Sleep hadn't come easy. Not at all really, and she'd tried to take advantage of the insomnia to think about Callie's dress. That had only made Serena anxious and lonely.

She fought the urge to throw herself against his chest and bawl about the ruined wedding dress for her friend's upcoming fairy-tale wedding. He would hold her and make her feel better. The way no one else could. And then she remembered. Kane wasn't into dresses, and he didn't believe in fairy tales.

She raised her coffee and took a sip. "Sure."

Kane placed his coffee cup on the table and sat across from her. He wore jeans, a green shirt and a brown leather jacket that made his eyes look hazel. His hair was damp as if straight from the shower. His razor stubble was gone, replaced by smooth skin she longed to feel rubbing against her cheek.

"Sleep well?" he asked.

"Not as well as I thought I would."

"Me, neither."

Clean and casual, he looked entirely too delectable. She wanted a taste. Instead she dug into another bite of her buttermilk pancakes with maple syrup.

Kane whistled. "That's some breakfast."

She eyed her plate of scrambled eggs, pancakes, bacon and fruit. "I was hungry."

"A couple of days of granola bars, honey-roasted peanuts, pretzels and crackers will make you crave a real breakfast."

"I wasn't tired of the food we had at the cabin." She remembered the many wrappers that had piled up during their meals. "I liked the cabin. Well, except for the wolves, the mice and the outhouse. There's something to be said for flush toilets."

His smile reached his eyes, and her heart beat faster. "You didn't go away."

"Excuse me?"

"The Serena I got to know at the cabin. I thought she'd disappeared, especially after Super Serena wowed the media with her sparkling brilliance."

"Brilliance?"

"I needed sunglasses, Blondie."

She smiled at his use of the nickname. "I was trying to get through the press conference the best way I knew how."

The only way she knew how, by reverting to what she did best—putting on a perfect facade. Maybe Super Serena did exist.

"You did great," he said. "You're back in your element."

"I don't feel like it," she admitted. "I feel like the only scarlet and gold cap-sleeved on a rack of strapless diamond whites."

Kane raised his cup and took a sip. "That bad."

"You have no idea what I just said."

"Nope, but I could tell from your tone that you feel out of place and that matters to me."

"Why does it matter?"

"I like you."

"You like me?" Not good enough. "Like me how?"

A beat passed. "As I said at the press conference, you're my friend, Serena."

Her heart deflated a little even though being just friends made sense. As Audra would say, anything else wouldn't be logical. "You're mine, too, but…"

The word hung out there. She was afraid to say more. Still she might not get another chance. "What happened at the cabin…?"

"It was…"

"Nice?" she offered.

"Great."

"Yes, great," she admitted. "I didn't know how you felt."

"You know I like you, Blondie. I'm attracted to you, but we want different things."

"We do." And taking what happened at the cabin any further made no sense. Kane understood that. So did Serena. But the thought of never seeing him again…hurt.

"I just came in for a quick cup of coffee." He pushed back his chair. "So maybe I'll see you around."

A brush-off. "You planning a trip to Boston?" she asked lightly. Stupid question. He didn't plan.

His gaze met hers. "I could be."

Oh, heavens.

Friends, she reminded herself. They wanted different things. "Then I'll see you in Boston sometime."

He nodded once.

Her heart thudded. She couldn't wait.

"I've got an appointment with the Forest Service this morning about my plane." He stood. "Have a safe flight home."

She hated to see him go. "Good luck with your plane and, well, everything else."

He leaned over and kissed her on the forehead. Nothing more than a friendly brush of his lips. "Goodbye, Blondie."

"Bye, Kane."

He left the coffee shop and got into a nondescript blue sedan. As he backed out, he waved at her. She waved back.

Mr. Right, Mr. Right Now or Mr. Wrong, Serena didn't care. A sigh escaped from her lips. She hoped sometime came soon because she really wanted to see him again.

"Thank you." As Belle took her suitcase from Charlie at Logan International Airport in Boston, her hand brushed his. Tingles shot up her arm. She ignored them, the same way she paid no attention to the warmth settling over the center of her chest. "I don't know how I would have made it through without you…your friendship."

"I feel the same way." His gaze held hers, and her heart melted a little. "I'll give you and Serena a ride home."

His continued generosity touched Belle. She glanced at the restroom to see if Serena was out yet. "That's sweet of you, but Regina's husband, Dell, arranged for a limo to take us home."

Charlie's smile didn't reach his eyes. "Riding home in style."

"Serena deserves it."

He raised Belle's hand to his lips and kissed it. "So do you."

The heat in her cheeks matched the temperature of the blood racing through her veins. Blushing at her age? But she wasn't used to a man switching attention from one of the girls to her. Belle pulled her hand away from his and adjusted the purse strap on her shoulder.

"When can I see you again?" he asked.

She hesitated. Sure, he was an attractive and wealthy man. She'd enjoyed his company, they'd relied on each other during the stress-filled days and become closer. But now that the crisis was over, seeing him again might not be such a good idea. He was a nice man, but Belle didn't want to lead him on.

"That hard to answer, huh?" he added, humor lacing his words.

Maybe she shouldn't put too much thought into the decision. Belle smiled. "Give me a call, darlin'."

That was the best she could come up with right now.

Anticipation filled his brown eyes. "I will."

His lighthearted grin took ten years off his face. Her heart sank. She was already nine years older than Charlie. Add ten to nine and… She didn't want to think about the total.

He wrapped his arms around her and squeezed. His hug shouldn't have surprised her. They'd held and comforted each other in Idaho. Support was no longer necessary, yet a part of Belle didn't want it to end.

Uh-oh. She was acting like one of her girls when they met a new beau. Maybe this wasn't such a good idea.

She stepped out of Charlie's embrace. "I need to get Serena home. She looks as if she hasn't slept a wink and she's been so quiet. Do you know if anything happened between her and Kane that we don't know about?"

"Kane said they were friends."

"Friends like us?" Belle asked, wondering if Serena was keeping more secrets to herself.

"He didn't elaborate, but I think you know I want to be more than your friend, Belle."

She nodded. The way Kane looked at Serena reminded Belle of the way Charlie looked at her. The elder Wiley was a true gentleman, but the younger seemed to be more of a ladies' man. That could spell only one thing for Belle's already heartbroken young designer—T-R-O-U-B-L-E.

CHAPTER TEN

THE Monday after she'd returned to Boston on a thankfully uneventful flight, Serena sat in her studio trying to reconstruct Callie's dress, but nothing seemed to be working. Serena didn't have enough of the diamond white delustered satin left so she was using a regular white satin instead. The fabric, however, had bluer overtones and didn't drape as well as the original. The seed and bugle beads seemed to disappear against the satin's higher sheen. Should she use more crystals or a tinted lace? Both would change the look of the dress. Who was she kidding? The fabric already did. Maybe she should come up with a new design.

Tossing a piece of embellished tulle onto her worktable, Serena glanced at the giant calendar hanging on the wall. Twelve days until Callie and Jared's wedding. Two fittings would need to be scheduled in. Time for alterations in between. Serena had the Brodeur bridesmaids flying into town this weekend for measurements. She couldn't forget about the Craggin fitting scheduled for Tuesday and the Cross fitting scheduled for next Thursday. And then there was Callie's surprise shower on Wednesday night. Serena rubbed her pounding head.

Closing her eyes, she imagined Callie's finished wedding gown but saw the cabin instead. Serena could smell smoke and pine and hear the rattle of wind against the windows. If only she could be there with Kane, instead of here alone.

Not good. Serena opened her eyes and glanced around her studio. How come what she'd always wanted no longer seemed…enough?

A knock sounded on the door separating the studio from the rest of the shop. She checked her watch. Her next appointment was over an hour away. "Come in."

"I brought in a new cake to taste." Pink and purple chopsticks, most likely painted by Natalie's twin daughters, secured the pile of blond hair on the top of her head. In her well-worn jeans and blue sweater that matched the color of her eyes, she looked more like a college student than a mom and talented cake maker. "It's chocolate."

"My favorite."

"I know." Natalie never brought cake into the studio due to all the white fabric. The petite baker hopped up and sat on a nearby stool. "How's it going?"

Serena ignored the calendar and forced a smile. "Good."

"You've been working so hard since you got back."

"Lots of winter weddings. And Callie's gown." Serena picked up one of the bodice panels. "I wish…"

"What do wish?"

"Nothing really. Do-overs aren't possible."

"A lot of us wish they were." Natalie sighed. "What would you change if you could?"

"Nothing."

"Come on," Natalie challenged. "You're the one who brought it up. There has to be something."

If Serena could be herself with Kane, maybe she should try to be more honest with her closest friends.

"I would have told you all about Rupert as soon as it happened." She looked down at her worktable. "I should have told you all."

"You did finally tell us the truth and answered our questions," Natalie said. "That couldn't have been easy for you."

"Or any of you." Serena looked up at her. "I really am sorry. I just didn't want to disappoint any of you."

Natalie smiled softly. "Just remember, next time we're here for you. We love you."

"I will."

"You'd better." Natalie sounded every bit a mom. "Now go get a slice of cake."

"I'd love one." Serena knew the baker, a diabetic, couldn't taste her own creations and relied on the Belles for their opinions. "And thanks, Nat."

"For what?"

"For being my friend."

"Anytime. That's what the Belles are for." Natalie beamed. "I'm going to see if Audra wants a slice."

Serena made her way into the reception area. The front desk was empty. She picked up a slice of chocolate cake with a raspberry fruit filling.

As she raised a forkful of cake, the scents of chocolate and icing filled her nostrils. Okay, things could be a lot worse right now. She took a bite. The chocolate flavor exploded in her mouth. The not-too-sweet raspberry filling complemented the cake and icing perfectly.

As she ate, the doorbell rang. With a mouthful of cake, she opened the door. Kane stood on the porch in a pair of black pants, a black turtleneck and his brown leather jacket. She choked on the bite.

His dark eyes narrowed. "You okay, Blondie?"

She nodded, struggling to swallow. "Cake."

"Can I have a taste?"

Serena scooped a bite with her fork and fed it to him.

"That's the best cake I've ever tasted." He smiled at her.

Her heart thudded. And that's when she knew. She wasn't Kane's friend. She was in love with him. Even though she'd only known him for a few days, they had been the most intense days of her life. He was totally wrong for her and didn't fit any of her plans or her life, but she didn't care. All she wanted was to be with him.

That realization scared her to death.

"You look good," he said.

"Thanks." The appreciation in his eyes made her forget she'd been up half the night, hadn't showered this morning and wasn't wearing lip gloss. "How did things go with your plane?"

"I can't get it out of Gold Meadows until spring, but the insurance company declared it a total loss based on the pictures and the report write-up."

"Kane." She reached for him, but pulled back her arm. "I'm so sorry."

"No worries," he said. "I'll buy another."

"And fly away again."

He nodded.

"When do you plan to do that?" she asked lightly, trying to sound like it didn't matter to her.

"As soon as I can."

Serena felt as if her clothing had been stitched too tightly and she couldn't breathe. Not that she should be surprised. He'd never pretended to be anything but what he was.

He handed her a medium-size white shopping bag. "For you."

She peeked inside and saw white tissue paper.

"Go on," he urged.

Serena pushed aside the paper. Something gray and white was there. She pulled the stuffed animal out and smiled. "A wolf."

"A little something to remember your adventure in Gold Meadows."

She would never forget it. Or him. She cuddled the wolf. "That was so thoughtful of you. Thank you, Kane."

He hooked his thumb through a belt loop. "Do you have time for a cup of coffee?"

Yes. She wanted to see him even if things weren't perfect. *No.* He would just leave again, so why bother? "I, um, have an appointment in an hour and I should be working."

"My dad told me what happened to a few of your dresses."

"You've been talking to your dad?" she asked.

"I'm staying with him."

"Good." Maybe they could start working out some of their differences. That would be good for Kane and Charlie, too. She smiled. "He must be happy to have you around."

Kane shrugged. "If you've been working so much you probably need caffeine or something besides cake to eat."

"There's nothing wrong with cake."

"Nope, but you can't live on cake alone. You need coffee, too." He grinned. "Come on, I promise I won't keep you."

The problem was she wanted him to keep her. Forever. She swallowed hard.

"What do you say, Blondie?"

Serena wanted to say yes.

Maybe she could convince him that they would be good for each other. That he could find what he needed right here in Boston. Or maybe not. And he would fly off chasing his notion of freedom again. She stared at the wolf in her arms. "One cup, then I have to get back to work."

Walking on the sidewalk with Serena felt weird to Kane. The sounds of traffic on the street, the squeal of breaks and the blare of horns were a far cry from the snow-swallowed silence of the wilderness. The smells of exhaust and garbage made him miss the fresh pine and smoke scents. But he was happy to be with Serena. He'd missed her so much that when he'd seen the wolf in a store window in Missoula, he'd bought it for her without a moment's hesitation.

"We weren't gone that long," he said. "But I'm not used to being back in the real world yet."

"Me, neither." Serena looked up at him with big round sunglasses covering her eyes. She wore a trendy wool coat, black boots and a knee-length skirt. A multicolored cap covered her blond hair. "I never really paid attention to all the different noises in the city before, but now I really miss the quiet of the woods. I keep thinking about the cabin."

And he'd been thinking about her. Too much.

Like me how?

Serena's words and the look in her eyes at the restaurant that morning had haunted Kane for the past four days. He had thought being away from her would keep her out of his thoughts and off his mind.

Wrong.

Which was why he needed to see her. To prove to

himself these strong feelings for her meant nothing, that he was hooked on a silly fantasy, nothing more.

"So…" she said.

He stopped on the curb waiting for the light to change. "So you've been busy."

"Yes, the work keeps piling up." She shoved her gloved hands in her pockets, reminding Kane of when she had worn his gloves, and smiled. "It's been hard getting back into the swing of things, but I'm checking things off the To Do list."

Kane had wondered how she was managing since returning home. He'd pictured her in full coping, press-conference mode. Super Serena to the max. But he could see now, he'd been wrong about that.

Despite the usual perfection of her appearance and even a smile on her face, she looked tired and stressed and a little sad. Instead of those things making her less beautiful, they only made him care for her more.

Real, not fantasy.

Self-preservation told him to run away as fast as he could. He could find a new plane anywhere. But Kane knew how vulnerable Serena James was. He didn't want to hurt her.

They entered a corner coffeehouse where they ordered drinks to go. Serena picked up a sandwich, too.

"What's really wrong, Blondie?" he asked on the walk back to the shop. "You've got a smile on your face, but you don't look happy."

"What do you mean?" Her brows drew together. "I've got almost everything a girl could want. Of course I'm happy."

"I'm not buying it." He removed her glasses. "I see a woman who's tired and stressed."

"I worked late last night and forgot to eat dinner and breakfast." She flashed him a brilliant smile. "I'm a little hungry, but okay."

"Good thing you bought a sandwich." He placed the sunglasses back on her face. "But a person doesn't have to feel good to smile as long as they know how to flex their facial muscles. That's what my mom used to say when she was trying to get me to admit I'd had a bad day."

Serena sipped her latte. "Did it work?"

"Usually." Kane wished his mom was here so he could talk to her about Serena. "Why don't you just tell me what's going on? Unless you want me to start guessing."

"Please don't."

She sounded horrified at the thought. Chalk another one up to Mom. A smile pulled at his lips. "So…"

"The biggest thing right now is Callie's dress," Serena explained. "She's my friend and the florist at The Wedding Belles. Her dress was one that got ruined. Destroyed, actually. Her wedding is a week from Saturday and I'm not even close to having something ready so I can fit her for alterations."

"You need help."

"I can do it myself."

"Can you?" he asked. "Or is that Super Serena talking?"

"There is no Super Serena. Just me. And I can do it."

She sounded capable and sure of herself. He wasn't buying it. "You can do it if you don't sleep or eat or waste a single moment of time."

Her mouth formed a perfect *O*. "We hardly know each other, yet you seem to know me the best of all. How is that possible?"

"It's a gift." He studied her, trying to see beneath that perfect facade. "Let me help you."

She drew back. "You?"

The offer had been an impulse, but Kane liked hearing the sound of her laughter and knowing he'd been the reason for it. If worst came to worst, he'd get to spend some time with her. No regrets there. "Yeah, me."

"What do you know about wedding dresses?"

"Less than you know about planes," he admitted. "But I can be an extra pair of hands, a sounding board, someone to bring you food, whatever you need."

"Mr. Right Now?"

Oh, man. Kane rocked back on his heels. "If that's what you want."

She looked down at her coffee and he felt like a heel. She wanted so much more than he could give her.

"In any case—" she pressed her lips together and met his eyes "—you're leaving."

"I'm not leaving until I find a plane. The right plane. I have a few to look at, but what's a few extra days in Boston if I get to help you?"

Those baby blues of hers widened. "A few days."

The hope in her voice and the anticipation in her eyes slammed into him. Suddenly following through on his offer didn't seem such a good idea. Kane nodded anyway.

"Okay, then," she said. "You're hired."

When Kane had agreed to help Serena, he hadn't really known what he was getting himself into. He hadn't really cared. What had he promised her? A few days. No big deal.

But helping her out felt good. Things had remained platonic, too. He wasn't about to take advantage of her.

"Can you please move that one about three inches to the left," Serena asked.

But he'd never thought he'd be standing in one of

Boston's finest mansions hanging wedding dresses on the walls of the impressive dining room. "No problem."

And it wasn't.

He enjoyed seeing Super Serena in action. The way she took charge of the decorating for Callie's surprise wedding shower tonight reminded him of a military leader in action. Serena executed her orders with quick decisive steps. So far he'd strung wide satin ribbons around the dining room and now was hanging wedding dresses on fancy hangers with big bows.

He moved the dress he was holding the requested three inches. "How's this?"

"Perfect."

Her favorite word.

He had to admit Serena James was pretty damned perfect herself. Not that he planned to do anything about that.

Okay, Kane had feelings for her, but he wasn't about to hurt her, especially when she was going through such a hard time remaking that damned wedding dress. He would help her and then he would leave.

"There's one more gown," she said.

"Where do you want it?" he asked.

She pointed to the spot. He moved the stepladder and hung the dress.

Sure, he'd thought about taking things further. But there was no sense starting something he couldn't finish.

"How's that?" he asked.

"A little to the left."

He'd learned with the seven other dresses not to guess-timate. She'd only make him redo it. "How little?"

"An inch and a half."

Good thing he'd asked. Kane moved the dress, pleased with the work they'd done.

Serena impressed him. She'd transformed the dining room into the perfect setting for a bridal shower. No wonder people spoke about her creativity with awe. She really was something.

He climbed down from the stepladder. "What do you think?"

She spun around slowly, taking in each dress, all the ribbons, every bow. "It works."

"It's fantastic," he said. "And I'm a guy. I'm not supposed to notice stuff like this. Good job."

She smiled. "You, too." ·

"You deserve all the credit. You're the one who came up with the idea and told me what to do."

Something in her eyes changed. "You know, there's been something else I've been wanting to tell you to do ever since you came back."

"What?" he asked, intrigued.

"This." She leaned over and kissed him.

The feel of her mouth against his, her lips pressing and probing, sent his temperature skyrocketing. He'd been pretending that he hadn't wanted to kiss her. That she hadn't meant much to him.

But he had and she did.

She tasted sweet and warm as she moved her lips over his. He wanted more. Hell, he wanted all she was willing to give.

Kane brought his arm around her, running his fingers through her hair. He explored every inch of her mouth, and she his. He soaked up the feel and taste of her, kissing her as if there were no tomorrow. He felt as if he'd found the place where he belonged and he never wanted to leave again. He was finally home.

The kisses continued until she slowly and gently pulled away. Serena stared at him with wide eyes and swollen, thoroughly kissed lips.

"That's what you've been wanting to tell me to do since I came back?" he asked.

She lifted her chin. "Yes."

He smiled, as he brushed strands of her bangs that had fallen over her right eye. "You are so beautiful, so brave, so perfect."

"You think?"

"I know." He kissed her lightly on the lips. "I might have to stick around Boston a little while longer."

Her smile lit up her face. "There's nothing I'd like more."

At the monthly poker and margarita night, Serena glanced at the clock on the wall of Regina's kitchen. The guests should have arrived for Callie's surprise wedding shower.

Now all they had to do was get the bride-to-be into the dining room. Good thing Part B of Operation Poker Plan was already under way.

Audra flipped her long blond hair behind her shoulder. "I'm all-in, too."

Callie gasped as the pile of chips in the center grew taller. "The entire table is all-in? That's impossible."

Serena looked at her partners in crime—Audra and Regina. The other Belles—Natalie, Julie and Belle herself—were busy in the dining room.

"This doesn't make any sense. There aren't that many good hands." Callie's face scrunched. She studied the cards on the table. "Serena never goes all-in. Could it be a certain pilot is leading you to take more risks these days?"

"Maybe."

"You and hottie flyboy seem pretty chummy," Regina said.

"We're getting chummier." Serena took a sip of her margarita thinking about what had happened earlier. "I kissed him this afternoon."

"And?" Callie asked.

Serena got all tingly inside. "It was absolutely, positively toe-curling wonderful."

"I'd like to experience a kiss like that," Audra said. "That is, if I ever planned to date again."

"You will," Serena encouraged. "And I hope you find someone who makes your toes curl."

Callie's eyes softened. "It's nice to see you opening up and talking about Kane like this."

"It feels good," Serena admitted. "Hey, don't we need to see who wins this huge pot of chips?"

Regina nodded. "Let's see your cards, ladies."

Serena laid her pair of threes on the table. The other two had nothing but a couple of face cards.

"I can't believe you guys went all-in on those hands. It's as if you wanted to lose." Callie flipped over a full house. "I win."

"Great hand," Audra said.

Callie moved the stack of chips in front of her and took a sip from her frozen margarita. "Not a bad haul, but I can't believe how fast the game ended."

Serena nursed her own drink. She still had work to do and a part of her hoped Kane might stop by. She bit back a sigh. "Luck of the cards."

Callie shuffled the deck. "We have time for another game."

"How does the new buffet look in the dining room, Regina?" Audra asked.

"I'd like to see it," Serena added, not wanting to delay Part C of the evening's plan.

"Let's all go and see it." Regina stood.

"But then we're going to play some more." Callie picked up her drink and followed Audra. "This time next month things will be different. I'll be a married woman."

Regina led the way, surreptitiously picked up her camera from the kitchen counter on her way toward the dining room. She crossed the threshold first. Next came Audra. Then Callie.

"Surprise!" a group of twenty women yelled.

Flashes from Regina's camera blinded Serena, but she kept a smile on her face. The photos would go into a wedding shower album the photographer wanted to put together for their friend.

"How did you guys do all this?" Callie asked Serena.

"While we played poker, Belle, Natalie and Julie set up and snuck guests into the dining room."

Callie stared wide-eyed. "I can't believe how quiet everyone was."

Julie smiled. "Belle threatened some nasty Southern torture to anyone who so much as sneezed."

"We Southerners know how to control a crowd, darlin'," Belle said.

"I had no idea," Callie admitted. "Though everyone going all-in at once was a little strange. But it's all so wonderful. Look at those wedding dresses hanging on the walls. Amazing."

Regina handed Callie a fresh margarita. "Using the dresses as decorations was Serena's brilliant idea."

Serena appreciated the compliment. "Well, I couldn't exactly ask our florist and decorating idea generator for help, now could I? I had to come up with something on my own."

"The gown I wore when I married Matthew is next to the window," Belle said.

Callie turned and sighed. "Lovely."

"Dated, but still pretty and so little," Belle said. "There wasn't quite so much of me back then."

"We wouldn't want you any other way," Audra said, and the rest of the Belles agreed.

Belle sniffled. "What would I do without you girls?"

"I don't know what I'd do without any of you. Thank you." Callie blinked. "This is so much more than I ever imagined having."

Everyone knew Callie hadn't had the easiest of times, but things had changed for the better since she'd joined The Wedding Belles and fallen in love with Jared Townsend.

As Serena thought about Kane, she wiggled her toes. He didn't seem to be in any hurry to leave Boston. He wanted to help her. He'd kissed her back. That had to mean he had feelings for her, but she had to be patient. She couldn't force Kane to love her. She didn't want to force him to run, either. She just wanted him to tell her how he felt about her. She imagined her and Kane as a couple. Like Callie and Jared. The image filled her with warmth.

"A toast." Serena raised her glass. "To Callie and Jared. May their love for one another never stop growing. Even after the wedding, the honeymoon and the kids."

Everyone laughed.

"Kids?" Callie teased. "I may need another drink."

Serena continued. "Best wishes on your journey toward your happily ever after."

"Hear, hear!" The guests raised their margarita glasses. "To Callie and Jared."

"Thank you," Callie mouthed.

Nodding, Serena smiled, though celebrating was the last thing she should be doing right now. Callie trusted her to get the dress done, but Serena wouldn't have missed tonight for the world. Even if being here meant working another late night.

Her friend was worth it.

Callie deserved the perfect wedding gown for the perfect wedding. Serena wasn't about to let her down.

CHAPTER ELEVEN

BY SATURDAY night, Serena was overwhelmed and exhausted. She glanced at the clock. Nine o'clock. All she wanted to do was go to sleep. All she could do was work on Callie's wedding dress. If Serena finished the gown tonight, she could work on the embellishments tomorrow and be ready for a fitting on Monday. That would allow plenty of time for alterations.

Kane stood behind her and massaged her tense shoulders. "You're all bunched up, Blondie."

She almost moaned with relief. "It's been a long week, but you being here to help has made it better."

"I'm happy to help." He kissed her neck. "I was thinking I could spend the night here."

Her insides fluttered, then tensed. "Tonight?"

"I could take better care of you if I was on-site so to speak."

"No." The word rushed from her mouth. "I'm too busy, too distracted. I want your first night here to be perfect."

His mouth tightened. "Why does everything always have to be so perfect with you?"

Because that's how things should be when I tell you I love you. She couldn't tell him that. "It just does."

Great, she sounded like a little kid.

"I'm not trying to get you into bed, Blondie." His gaze held hers. "I'm only trying to take care of you the best way I know how."

She looked at the mannequin wearing Callie's almost finished dress. "Not tonight."

"Why not?"

"I don't have time."

"I'm not asking for your time. Just a space on your couch."

She shook her head. "I... That's not good enough."

He stepped away from her. "You mean I'm not good enough."

"I never said that."

"You didn't have to." The hurt in his voice clawed at her heart. "You're too busy chasing your vision of perfection to see something right and real in front of you. Can't you cut me some slack?"

"Slack?" Her voice rose. Serena had thought Kane understood her, but he didn't. He couldn't. "I have to finish the dress."

"Or kill yourself trying." He picked up a piece of lace and waved it in the air. Though the lace was white, she didn't think he was surrendering. "Is a dress worth all this? The sun will still rise tomorrow if you don't get it done."

"I have to have it done."

"Then ask for some help." He dropped the fabric. Tenderness filled his eyes. "Your friends would be here in a heartbeat."

"Callie trusts me. She's counting on me," Serena explained, feeling as if everything she held dear was about to unravel. "I have it under control."

"I'm sorry, Blondie, but you don't."

She stiffened.

"You've got to stop pretending. Look at the toll this is taking on you. Your health. Your life. It's destroying you. I won't let you keep this up."

"You won't let me?" No one told her what to do. Her temper flared. "I can do this. I will do this. I don't need anybody's help. Not even yours."

His expression shuttered. "Well, thanks a lot."

She stared at the wedding dress, her heart aching as if she'd lost her best friend. "What do you want me to say?"

"I'm sorry would be a good start."

She'd thought he accepted her for who she was, not who he wanted her to be.

"Why?" Pain, raw and jagged, sliced through her. "So you can get in your plane and fly away with no hard feelings? That's what you do best, isn't it? Take off when you don't get what you want?"

"You're way off base. This has nothing to do with me." His gaze hardened, accused. "Nothing will ever be perfect enough for you, Serena. I don't know why I've stuck around and even tried."

Emotion clogged her throat. Her stomach clenched. She couldn't breath.

Everything she'd thought about, dreamed about and planned for was coming to an end. And she felt helpless to stop it.

She'd known what Kane Wiley was like from the very beginning. He'd even told her himself. The quintessential Mr. Wrong, but she'd pretended that he could be her Mr. Right.

Well, he was right about something. It was time to stop pretending.

"Then I guess," she said, her voice trembling, "you'd better go."

* * *

Kane sat in his rented car, his hands on the steering wheel to keep them from shaking. He needed to calm down before driving away.

He took a deep breath, unsure what had just happened.

Why? So you can get in your plane and fly away with no hard feelings. That's what you do best, isn't it? Take off when you don't get what you want?

Serena had it all wrong. This wasn't about him. He hadn't wanted a relationship. He avoided them like bad fuel, but both had found him in Seattle.

Now he was sitting in his car staring at a brightly lit flat. Outside looking in. That's how Kane usually liked things. Distant, removed, safe. But at this moment he felt none of those things. Kane felt as if someone had yanked his entire life from him. His home, everything he'd wanted, was gone yet again.

That hurt.

And made him feel…stupid.

When was he ever going to learn? Love equaled pain. No two ways about it.

Maybe he shouldn't have pushed her when she was already tired and stressed out, but her mood didn't affect the basic situation.

Little Miss Perfection wasn't going to change. Super Serena was back and not going away. She wanted her perfect life and he didn't fit in. He'd been a fool to think that he could or that she would let him.

Kane should have known better.

Next time… There wasn't going to be a next time.

Heartbroken over what had just happened, Serena sat on the middle of her living room floor staring at the dress she'd been working on for days. Over a week actually.

Tears filled her eyes, but she blinked them away. She wanted to cry over Kane. She wanted to cry hard, but still had too much to do.

She focused on the gown. Even with the new fabric, Callie's dress, almost complete, wasn't coming out right. Serena had been ignoring the truth, but couldn't any longer. Her broken heart splintered more. She was going to have to start over. Which meant she would never be able to make Callie the kind of dress she deserved to wear on the most special day of her life.

Serena cradled her head in her hands.

Her fault. She'd failed. She'd let her friend down in the worst possible way.

Tears stung Serena's eyes, but surrounded by yards of delicate fabrics and lace, she kept them at bay. Not that she had time to use the fabric to make a new dress from scratch now.

What was she going to do? How was she going to tell Callie?

Serena hugged her knees.

All her plans had disintegrated, leaving her nothing to fall back on, nothing to hold on to or reach for. How could everything go from perfect to disaster so quickly?

You're too busy chasing your vision of perfection to see something right and real in front of you.

Kane's words rushed back to Serena. Her shoulders slumped. She had just been trying to do the best she could. What was wrong with wanting a perfect life or a perfect man or a perfect wedding dress?

Perfect wedding dress. Serena repeated the word. She straightened and stood. Maybe…

She padded her way to the hall closet and opened the door. Hanging there, wrapped in plain muslin, was her almost-completed dream wedding gown. A perfect wedding dress. For her perfect marriage to the absolutely wrong for her Rupert.

She uncovered the gown.

Serena felt no excitement, no joy, no longing the way she had before. Her needing the dress had simply been a dream, a wish that hadn't come true. Chasing a vision— make that a clouded vision—of perfection, most definitely. She sighed.

But Callie's dream was very much alive. Her and Jared's happily ever after still existed. She deserved this gown to start her new life with her husband.

Not perfect. Not for Serena any longer.

But just right for Callie. And right here.

This gown would be the one.

Serena placed the dress on the mannequin. She grabbed her sketch pad, sat on the floor once again and drew how she wanted the completed dress to look. Not for her, but for Callie.

Thirty minutes later, Serena was ready to begin the transformation, but she'd learned her lesson. She couldn't do this on her own. She needed help to make sure she got this dress finished on time.

Just remember, next time we're here for you. We love you.

Serena knew exactly who to call—The Wedding Belles. Her friends would understand. They would help her. Nothing, not time or tiredness, would stop them from creating a spectacular wedding gown for Callie.

The oohs and aahs filled the dress design studio on Monday night after Julie had put out the calligraphy-script Closed sign and locked the front door. The only question remaining was whether the bride liked the gown or not. Serena held her breath.

"It's absolutely perfect." Tears glistened in Callie's eyes as she stared at her reflection in the three-panel mirror. She spun around on the carpeted platform. "I love it even more than the first dress."

So did Serena. She hadn't let her friend down.

The dress, the one she'd spent weeks designing and stitching with an "I do" in mind, was no longer hers. Each stitch, each bead, each crystal may have been sewn with love in mind, but not the forever kind. The friend kind. She'd turned the dress into Callie's dream gown. Sleek and neat. Not at all what Serena had planned for herself, but perfect for Callie.

Belle clasped her hands to her chest. "You are the most beautiful bride."

Callie's smile lit up her face. "You say that to all the brides."

"Because it's true."

She stared at her reflection in the mirror. "Thank you, Serena."

"Don't thank me." Serena had learned her lesson in time to save Callie's wedding gown, but not in time to salvage her relationship with Kane. "For the past two days, we all worked on the dress."

"Thank you, everyone." Callie's voice bubbled with excitement.

Everyone spoke at the same time. Laughed. Hugged.

Callie looked at Serena. "Is it horrible if I say I'm glad you got stuck in the wilderness and the other dress got ruined?"

"Not at all," Serena said.

"I know Kane has been a big help to you. I want to thank

him." Callie glowed the way only a bride could. "Is he around?"

"I haven't heard from him." The honest answer tore Serena's heart in two. "I think he might have left Boston."

The studio went dead quiet. All six pairs of sympathetic eyes focused on Serena.

"I've seen how he looks at you, darlin'." Belle touched her shoulder. "He'll be back."

Serena knew he wasn't coming back. She'd wanted to apologize after all he'd done for her. For the past two days, she'd tried calling him both on his cell phone and at Charlie's. He hadn't returned any of her messages.

"It's okay," she said to her friends.

And it was. Or would be. Someday.

Kane had made his choice, and so had Serena. He didn't want her if she didn't behave the way he wanted, but she was tired of trying to please everyone all the time. She wasn't going to do it any longer. Especially for someone who ran away from commitment, the very thing she wanted most of all.

She couldn't be what he wanted, and he couldn't give her what she wanted. That, unfortunately, was the bottom line.

"She's a beauty, son," Charlie said about the business jet Kane wanted to buy two days later. "But have you thought this through?"

"I'm a pilot. Flying is how I make my living. I need a plane."

"Do you want to go back to that lifestyle, flying here and there, never staying in one place, with one person, for long?"

"I never left that life, Dad." Kane stared at the inch-thick sales contract. His grandfather had guaranteed what the insurance payout wouldn't cover. The only thing missing—Kane's signature on the paperwork. "I like my freedom."

"You can change how you live and still experience freedom."

Kane thought about Serena with her wide blue eyes and big, warm smile. He'd been willing to try, but she hadn't been willing to accept the man he'd tried so desperately to be for her. "I don't need to change anything."

"I used to think that way," Charlie said quietly. "After your mother…"

Kane looked up from the contract. "After Mom what?"

His father stared down at his shoes. "I loved your mother so much. She was my life. After she died, I missed her so much and I wasn't ready to face what had happened. I wasn't ready to change. I liked being married. I liked having someone there."

"So you married Evangeline."

Charlie nodded. "I was looking for a replacement more than anything. I know it hurt you, Kane."

"It did." A ball of emotion clogged his throat. "I guess I'd been in denial or something, but when you got married it made Mom's death seem more real. I finally had to accept she wasn't coming back. I wasn't ready to do that. I couldn't understand how you were ready to do that so quickly."

"Losing your mother was the hardest thing I've ever had to go through. But worse, I lost you, too," Charlie admitted. "I hope you can forgive me someday."

Kane didn't want to forgive. Holding on to the grudge—his anger—was easier than opening himself up to more hurt. But he knew his mother would have wanted him to at least hear his father out. "I'm listening."

"Marrying Evangeline was a mistake. I thought I loved her, but I didn't. I should have listened to you. I should have listened to a lot of people. I'm so very sorry, son." The sincerity in his father's voice struck a chord deep inside Kane. "I don't know if I'll ever love another woman the way I loved your mother. That doesn't mean I can't love a different way. There is someone I would like to pursue a relationship with if she'd have me, but I want your blessing this time."

"Are you talking about Belle?"

"Yes."

Kane took a deep breath and exhaled slowly. A part of him understood what his father was talking about. The other part still hurt. But holding on to his anger made little sense. He couldn't change what had happened. Not with his dad. Not with his mother. "If that's who you care for, go for it, Dad."

"Thank you, son," Charlie said, his voice grateful. "What about you and Serena?"

"It's complicated."

"Love always is."

Love?

"I tried to ignore your mother's death and live my life the way I always had. But I learned you have to face things head-on even if it's not easy. There's no avoiding the bad stuff. If you don't do it now, you'll only have to do it later."

His father's words sunk in. Had Kane been avoiding whatever went wrong in his life or getting upset when he didn't get his way?

So you can get in your plane and fly away with no hard feelings. That's what you like to do best, isn't it? Take off when the going gets tough?

Serena's words played in his mind. He thought about

his mother's death, his dad's second marriage, so many other things including Serena herself. She was right. He had run away. And he was doing it again.

"No matter what you decide, I love you." Charlie patted Kane's shoulder. "I'll always be here for you, son."

And that's what it was all about, he realized. Being there for those you cared about. Kane didn't want to spend his entire life leaving on a plane, flying from place to place. He remembered the home his parents had created for him, the love inside the walls.

Something so good wasn't easy to make happen. There were no guarantees, and the hard stuff required work. He'd avoided that all these years, but he was finally ready. He hoped he wasn't too late.

"Thanks, Dad," Kane said. "I'm sorry it took us so long to talk about this."

Charlie smiled. "We have plenty of time ahead of us."

"Just not right now." Kane moistened his dry lips. "Could you give me a lift?"

"Where to?"

"Wherever Serena might be, but we may need to make a stop or two on the way."

"Come on." Charlie headed down the stairs of the plane. "You navigate, and I'll drive."

Kane preferred being behind the wheel, but this time he'd happily sit in the passenger seat. "Let's go, Dad."

Serena cleaned up the mess in her living room, piling the fabric, lace, tulle and beading into a box. Once this stuff was back at the studio, she could put the entire wedding dress fiasco behind her. Too bad she couldn't do the same with Kane.

Kane.

Tears welled in her eyes. Serena hadn't known him that long, but she'd never experienced such emptiness, such loneliness since he'd been gone. Her heart felt as if all the blood had been squeezed out. Every beat hurt. She picked up the stuffed wolf from the couch.

How had she come to this? All her plans in ashes. Her plans...

Serena nearly laughed. Her plans hadn't been worth much. They hadn't kept her from falling in love with Mr. Wrong. She hugged the wolf.

Her heart wanted Kane still. No one else would do, even though he could never give her the kind of love and commitment she wanted. The truth cut deep, the raw wound threatening to swallow her whole. She wiped tears from the corners of her eyes.

Pathetic.

She'd wanted to be loved so badly, to have a family of her own, that she had been willing to engineer her future, plan everything, including the man she wanted to marry. She set the wolf down. At least she'd recognized the trap and wouldn't be caught in it again.

If only...

No. Serena wasn't looking back. She didn't want to look forward, either. She needed to stop planning and start living.

A knock sounded at her front door.

Serena wasn't expecting anyone. She picked up a tissue and blew her nose.

Another knock.

Go away.

And another.

The doorbell rang.

Fed up, Serena tossed the tissue in the garbage can and stormed to the door. "This had better be important."

She threw open the door and saw...

"Kane."

Tears exploded from her eyes.

"Serena?" he asked, his voice filled with concern.

She must look a fright. No makeup, unwashed hair, grungy clothes and red, puffy eyes. "Yes?"

"Seeing you like this..." He wiped the tears from her face with his thumb and led her inside, closing the door behind him. "I'm sorry. I shouldn't have left like that. I should have returned your calls, but you were right. Anytime something doesn't go right, I run away. I may think I'm chasing freedom, but all I'm doing is holding on to grudges and not looking back because it hurts too much."

She stared at him, shocked yet hopeful. She wanted to believe him.

His gaze lingered, practically caressed. "You and I aren't so different, Blondie."

"I'm sorry, too," Serena said, her eyes locked on his. "You were right about me. I get so focused on a goal I ignore everything else, every other possibility, including what's right in front of my face. Whether it's a wedding dress or..."

Choked up, she couldn't continue.

"We like having control of a situation, but when we don't, it's damn difficult." Kane inhaled sharply. "When my mother died, I had no control over anything. One minute I was trying to help my father, then the next thing I knew he was dating, engaged and remarried. I did the only thing I could. I left. I'm tired of leaving, Serena."

Her eyes met his. "But you said that's what you wanted to do. You want freedom—"

"I did, but freedom is no longer enough."

Serena was almost afraid to ask, but she had to know. "What do you want now?"

"You."

The air whooshed from her lungs. She struggled to breathe, to think.

"But flying is your life," she managed.

He smiled. "My hobby is flying. Loving you is my life."

Her heart melted. Her knees nearly gave way.

"I don't care if we're in Boston or stranded in the wilderness, whether you're designing wedding gowns or gathering firewood, I want to be with you. And I mean you, whoever you want to be. Serena, Super Serena or Blondie."

Serena touched her hand to her heart that seemed to be dancing to a tune of its own. "I don't know what to say."

"You don't have to say anything." The sincerity of his voice brought a lump to her throat. "I love you, Serena James."

The words she'd wanted to hear. She'd waited to hear them. But she'd had it all wrong. No special plans were necessary to say those words. The words themselves were perfect no matter when or where they were spoken. She swallowed. Hard. "I love you, too."

Kane pulled her toward him and kissed her. He kissed her lips, her cheeks, her neck. She felt as if he were kissing her heart and her soul. She couldn't be happier, feel more complete.

"I always had to be the good girl, never disappoint, so I put on this facade, always doing the right thing, saying the right words, never deviating from my plan. And that worked. Until I met you."

She pulled back and gazed into his eyes.

"I needed to give Callie the chance for the kind of wedding I always wanted, with a dress she'd always remember, but pushing myself to my limit took its toll on my time, my temper…and us. I learned my lesson though. When I finally realized I couldn't finish the dress myself, I called my friends, but by then you were…"

Gone.

The unspoken word echoed between them.

"I'm here now."

"Yes, you are." A peace filled her. "I finally realized I don't always have to be Super Serena all the time. I don't always have to do the right thing. In fact, I've learned I can be incorrect about what's right for me, especially about something very important."

"What's that?" he asked.

"Who was Mr. Wrong and who is Mr. Right."

His smile crinkled the corners of his eyes. "Who might that be?"

She stood on her tiptoes and kissed him hard on the lips.

"You are creative, smart, generous and beautiful, Blondie." His rich laughter wrapped itself around her heart. "I love you."

Joy filled her heart and overflowed. "I love you, too."

"Just to prove I mean what I said—" he dropped down on one knee and pulled something from his pocket "—will you marry me?"

She stared at the small glass slipper he held with his fingers. Inside was a simple, elegant diamond ring. She knew in her heart this was right. Not only was this the beginning of their fairy tale, but the start of a much better life, a life full of love.

"This ring belonged to my mother," he said. "It probably has to be resized. Or if you don't like it, I can buy you another. I want it to be perfect."

Serena put her fingers over his mouth. She didn't need to look at the ring. All she had to see was the love in Kane's eyes, real and right in front of her. "It's perfect. I love it."

"Does that mean—?"

"Yes." Her insides tingled. She had never felt so content or fulfilled in her life. "I love you. I would be honored to marry you, Kane Wiley. Or should I call you Mr. Right?"

"Call me whatever you want." He picked her up and twirled her around. "I don't care as long as we're together."

She laughed. "You know this means I have to design another wedding dress."

He set her down. "I can't wait to see what you come up with for yourself."

Thinking about standing at the altar with Kane at her side, Serena smiled. "Neither can I."

EPILOGUE

November 22nd

THE Castle at Boston University, a Tudor Revival Mansion, looked stately with its ivy-covered exterior. The interior matched expectations from the outside with its regal columns, inviting fireplace, crystal chandelier and wall of arched windows. The perfect space for a wedding reception, especially with the Belles in charge.

Callie and Jared's wedding was going off without a hitch. No detail had been overlooked. Guests enjoyed champagne cocktails and passed appetizers while the wedding party had photographs taken. An elegant catered sit-down dinner was served followed by the cake, a four-tiered white chocolate cake with raspberry filling decorated with Callie's favorite flower, the stargazer lily. Taking her cue from the monthly poker nights and not one to be totally traditional, Callie had made memorable center-pieces for each of the round linen-covered tables by filling extra-large margarita glasses with stargazer lilies and adding a piece of snake grass for the stirrer.

Now that the food and cake had been served, Belle and Julie, the only two Belles not members of the wedding party, removed their headsets and joined the others to watch Callie sing a romantic ballad to her husband on the DJ's karaoke machine. She swayed with the music, the yards of shantung silk of her gown swishing back and forth as she sang her heart out. Callie might have once believed Mr. Right didn't exist, but no one could mistake the love in her eyes and in her voice now.

Listening to her talented friend sing about believing in fairy tales brought a sigh to Serena's lips. A happy ending was in store for her friend. Serena couldn't be more pleased. She knew exactly how Callie felt about Jared because Serena felt the same way about Kane.

She leaned back against him, resting against his strong chest as if she'd been doing it her entire life. He wrapped his arms around her, and his warm breath caressed her neck. "Is this the kind of wedding you want to have?"

Once upon a time, Serena would have answered yes without hesitation, but now…now that she'd experienced a love so wonderful, so right, she no longer knew what kind of wedding she wanted. Or, to be honest, cared.

"As long as we say 'I do' and sign on the dotted line, it doesn't matter how we get married. The details aren't important." Serena stared at her hand, at the four-pronged set diamond solitaire engagement ring that had belonged to Kane's late mother. "What matters is how much I love you and what happens after the wedding."

"Have I told you how much I love you?" Kane whispered.

"About ten minutes ago."

"I won't wait so long the next time."

Serena smiled as Kane kissed her neck.

After Callie finished her song, Jared picked up his bride and kissed her, to the delight of the clapping audience.

"You really can't sing?" Kane asked Serena.

"Nope, but I still sing in the shower."

He grinned. "That's a performance I can't wait to see."

"Don't you mean hear?"

Kane whistled a little ditty.

Natalie's twins, Rose and Lily, ran across the dance floor in their matching flower girl dresses. They looked sweet and innocent in their white dresses with pink and cranberry ribbons, but the two were always up to some sort of mischief.

"I hope our children look exactly like you," Kane said, his voice full of warmth and love.

The DJ made an announcement asking all single women to come onto the dance floor. Serena laced her fingers with Kane's and turned to Audra and Natalie. "You two had better get out there."

"Looks like we're the only single Belles left, Natalie," Audra said.

The baker smiled. "Don't forget Belle."

"The six of us couldn't drag her out here." Natalie stepped forward two feet. "Let's not disappoint Callie. There are enough single women we won't have to worry about catching the bouquet way back here."

"Good," Audra said. "Because I'd rather catch the flu than the bouquet."

Natalie stared lovingly at her twin daughters, standing front and center, eager to catch the bouquet. "Me, too."

Callie stood with her back to the crowd and held the bouquet up in the air for all to see. Long stems of pink and white stargazers were tied with three neatly tailored bands of cranberry ribbon trimmed with clear crystals that looked like buttons, coordinating with the ones on her gown. Crystal accents stood up a half inch between each bloom throughout the bouquet. Callie wound up her arm as if she were pitching a fastball for the Red Sox and let her bouquet fly. Over the heads of the reaching women and right into the arms of...

Natalie.

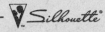

SPECIAL EDITION™

NEW YORK TIMES BESTSELLING AUTHOR

DIANA PALMER

A brand-new Long, Tall Texans novel

HEART OF STONE

Feeling unwanted and unloved, Keely returns to Jacobsville and to Boone Sinclair, a rancher troubled by his own past. Boone has always seemed reserved, but now Keely discovers a sensuality with him that quickly turns to love. Can they each see past their own scars to let love in?

Available September 2008 wherever you buy books.

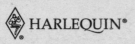

Lawyer Audrey Lincoln has sworn off
love, throwing herself into her work
instead. When she meets a much younger
cop named Ryan Mercedes, all her logic
is tossed out the window, and Ryan is
determined that he will not let the issue
of age come between them. It is not until
a tragic case involving an innocent child
threatens to tear them apart that Ryan
and Audrey must fight for a way to
finally be together....

Look for

TRUSTING RYAN
by Tara Taylor Quinn

*Available July
wherever you buy books.*

HARLEQUIN
More Than Words

"Changing the world,
one baby at a time."

—**Sally Hanna-Schaefer,** real-life heroine

*Sally Hanna-Schaefer is a Harlequin More Than Words
award winner and the founder of **Mother/Child Residential Program.***

Discover your inner heroine!

HARLEQUIN
More Than Words

"There are moms. There are angels. And then there's Sally."

—**Kathleen O'Brien**, author

*Kathleen wrote "Step by Step," inspired by Sally Hanna-Schaefer, founder of **Mother/Child Residential Program**, where for over twenty-six years Sally has provided support for pregnant women and women with children.*

Look for "*Step by Step*" in
More Than Words, Vol. 4,
available in April 2008 at eHarlequin.com
or wherever books are sold.

SUPPORTING CAUSES OF CONCERN TO WOMEN
WWW.HARLEQUINMORETHANWORDS.COM

MTW07SH2

HIGH-SOCIETY SECRET PREGNANCY

Park Avenue Scandals

Self-made millionaire Max Rolland had given up on love until he meets socialite fundraiser Julia Prentice. After their encounter Julia finds herself pregnant, but a mysterious blackmailer threatens to use this surprise pregnancy and ruin his reputation. Max must decide whether to turn his back on the woman carrying his child or risk everything, including his heart....

Don't miss the next installment of the Park Avenue Scandals series—
Front Page Engagement
by Laura Wright—
coming in August 2008
from Silhouette Desire!

Always Powerful, Passionate and Provocative.

HARLEQUIN *Romance*

Coming Next Month

Explore the rugged scenery of the Scottish Highlands, share the joys of first pregnancies and escape to the scorching heat of the desert this July in Harlequin Romance®!

#4033 PARENTS IN TRAINING by Barbara McMahon
Unexpectedly Expecting!
How exciting to finally have that longed-for baby! Concluding the inspiring duet, pregnant Annalise can't wait for babies with her husband. But although Dominic adores his wife, he always thought theirs would be a perfect family of *two....*

#4034 NEWLYWEDS OF CONVENIENCE by Jessica Hart
Corporate wife Mallory promised her new husband a businesslike marriage—no messy emotions involved! But moving to the Scottish Highlands where she discovers he's rugged, capable and utterly gorgeous, Mallory thinks she might want to break the terms of their arrangement.

#4035 WINNING THE SINGLE MOM'S HEART by Linda Goodnight
The Wedding Planners
Single moms like Natalie need romance, too! In this captivating story, competitive Cooper Sullivan is at the top of his career—but seeing Natalie after so many years, he realizes the only thing he really wants to win is her heart!

#4036 ADOPTED: OUTBACK BABY by Barbara Hannay
Baby on Board
Nell thought she'd missed her chance to be a mom when she was forced to put her baby up for adoption as a teenager. Now, at age thirty-nine, she discovers she has a tiny grandson who needs her! And the baby's grandfather, Nell's former sweetheart Jacob, is back in town....

#4037 THE DESERT PRINCE'S PROPOSAL by Nicola Marsh
Desert Brides
Prince Samman *must* marry to be crowned King—but he rejects all his advisors' suggestions! He wants intelligent, independent Bria Green, who's determined the powerful prince won't get his way. But will the scorching heat of the desert change her mind?

#4038 BOARDROOM BRIDE AND GROOM by Shirley Jump
9 to 5
What's your idea of the perfect date? Gorgeous lawyer Nick certainly doesn't think a children's picnic with prim colleague Carolyn is his! Yet Carolyn intrigues him, and Nick starts to think he has never seen anyone more beautiful....

HRCNM0608